Lost in the
Canadian
Wilderness

Lost in the Canadian Wilderness

What happened to Louie Harris?

to Betty and Monty, whose lives have been an inspiration to us. By your collective intellect, activity and dignity you have redefined the meaning of 'growing older'. Love, Nancy Seefeldt Vern Seefeldt

Vern Seefeldt

Copyright © 2011 by Vern Seefeldt.
Cover design by Riccardo Capraro
Illustrations by Riccardo Capraro

Library of Congress Control Number: 2011903247
ISBN: Hardcover   978-1-4568-7795-8
             Softcover   978-1-4568-7794-1
             Ebook   978-1-4568-7796-5

All rights reserved. No part of this book may be reproduced or transmitted in any form or by any means, electronic or mechanical, including photocopying, recording, or by any information storage and retrieval system, without permission in writing from the copyright owner.

This is a work of fiction. Names, characters, places and incidents either are the product of the author's imagination or are used fictitiously, and any resemblance to any actual persons, living or dead, events, or locales is entirely coincidental.

This book was printed in the United States of America.

To order additional copies of this book, contact:
Xlibris Corporation
1-888-795-4274
www.Xlibris.com
Orders@Xlibris.com
93126

CONTENTS

Disclaimer 9
Acknowledgments 11
Introduction 11

Chapter 1. In Quest of a New Lifestyle 17
Chapter 2. A Questionable Partnership in
            North Dakota's Wheat Fields 25
Chapter 3. To Winnipeg, Prince Rupert, and Hazelton 49
Chapter 4. Selecting the Homestead 63
Chapter 5. Building the Cabin 75
Chapter 6. Success on the Trapline 83
Chapter 7. An Icy Bath in October 99
Chapter 8. Adventures with Wolves 107
Chapter 9. The Winter Bear 121
Chapter 10. Metonka Flees Her People 127
Chapter 11. Visitors in the Valley 149
Chapter 12. Louie Is Missing 159
Chapter 13. Barney Leaves the Homestead without Louie 171

Postnote 191

Dedication

There are countless individuals to whom I am indebted for making this journey possible, but for this occasion I have limited the expression of gratitude to members of my immediate family. Special thanks are extended to: my father, Barney, who is the central character of this book, and my mother, Ella, who installed in their children the morality, ethical behavior and industry to survive in a world that was to become far different than the one in which they lived and one they could not have imagined during our childhood; my wife, Nancy, my best friend and companion for fifty-four years, who never really understood the need for numerous hunting and fishing trips, but was always there to welcome me after each safe return; daughter, Lynne, the consummate teacher and proof-reader, whose editorial comments greatly improved the readability of this book; son, John, for calling attention to the omissions and inconsistencies in the book that required adjustments. His skill as a hunter far surpasses mine and rivals that of his grandfather. Barney would have been proud; granddaughter, Kayla, and grandson, Ross, neither of whom has the literary preference for the content of this book, but whose academic achievements and lives as individuals have been a source of pride to their parents and grandparents; son-in-law Jesse, and daughter-in-law Karen, who have enriched our lives immeasurably as additions to our family; sister, Maxine, Green Bay's most ardent Packer fan, and matriarch of the family, who keeps the home fires burning; brothers Ralph, Gene and Earl, all of whom inherited from our father the love of nature and the joy of being in the outdoors.

Disclaimer

The dates, events and locations in this book are written exactly as they were told to the author by his father. However, names of all individuals, except Barney, are pseudonyms to protect the identity of persons involved in the events described herein. The word **Indian** is used in the narrative because that term was commonly used by the government officials and residents of Prince Rupert in 1925 with reference to the native people who inhibited northern British Columbia. The author is aware that such terms as Native People, Indigenous People, Native Americans and specific tribal names such as Tagish, Inland Tlingit and Kaska are currently preferred, but for purposes of authenticity, the term Indian is used in the narrative.

Acknowledgments

My adventures in the forests, woodlots, lakes, rivers and streams of this great land have been enriched by those who have shared these excursions with me. The true meaning of companionship, as expressed by courage, perseverance, support and generosity, often comes to the fore during extreme conditions. The following individuals-sportsmen all—have demonstrated the true meaning of companionship:

Jim Aird, Ron Bacon, Loran Bieber, Jeff Branch, Michael Branch, Gene Brown, Vernon Brown, Russ Bruce, Dave Cannon, Shawn Cannon, JC Clyma, Joey Cvengros, Mike Cvengros, Jerry Cvengros, Marv Elliott, Gordon Guyer, John Haubenstricker, Don Herrmann, Roger Hoopengarner, Ralph Hurley, Gordon Jensen, Jay Kim, Dennis Lankos, Scott McDonald, Gale Mikles, Henry Montoye, Jim Moore, Chuck Niemeyer, Ken Niemeyer, Kurt Niemeyer, Roy Niemeyer, John Nord, Joe Northrup, Chris Olson, Herb Olson, Scott Olson, Lavern Polzin, Art Radtke, Ken Reeder, Gideon Robarge, Robert Schmitz, Steve Schmitz, Charlie Seefeldt, Ervin Seefeldt, Roger Seefeldt, Fred Steffen, Paul Vogel and Ken Wagner.

This book is written as a tribute to my father, Bernhard (Barney) Herman William Seefeldt (1897–1973), who was born at a time when his home in Grover, Wisconsin, was very much a wilderness area. Wolves, bears, and coyotes preyed on the livestock that was left unsupervised. Forests and undrained swamps stood in the way of ambitious immigrant farmers, who had been led astray by advertisements offering countless acres of tillable land, available for anyone willing to cultivate the soil. Roads into the homesteads consisted of one-lane passageways, lined with trees and underbrush that had escaped the lumbermen's saws.

Born in a log cabin built by his father on the cutover ground left barren by the great Peshtigo fire of October 8, 1871, Barney grew up as the second youngest of eleven children. His parents emigrated from Pomerania, Germany, setting out for the United States by sailboat from Bremerhaven, Germany, in November 1855. After six weeks at sea, they arrived in New York Harbor in the cold of December to seek affordable land wherever it was still available. Disappointed by the high real estate prices in New York, but encouraged by the prospect of land in Wisconsin, the emigrants traveled up the Hudson River to Albany, then by steamboat on the Erie Canal to Buffalo, and then by ship on the Great Lakes to Menominee, Michigan. Land availability at $1.25 per acre in Grover township, Wisconsin, twenty miles from Menominee, prompted Carl Seefeldt, Barney's grandfather, to purchase eighty acres of depleted pinery, with the intention of extracting the huge pine stumps in readiness for farming the land.

The German-speaking community of Grover, Wisconsin, an area also referred to as the Lower Sugar Bush, so named because of the numerous maple trees from which the settlers made maple syrup, established its priorities by building their community church (St.

John's Evangelical Lutheran Church) in 1880 and the first school in the southwest corner of what is now Marinette County (Behnke School) in 1900. Low German (plattdeutsch) was spoken in social settings, but high German (hochdeutsch) was spoken in parochial schools and religious services, only to be overridden in 1890 when the Wisconsin legislature passed a law requiring all elementary schools in the state, whether public, private, or parochial, to teach "reading, writing, arithmetic, and United States history" in the English language. Despite the law, many of the religious groups continued to offer their instruction in German. For example, Barney's religious confirmation, in 1911, was conducted in the German language.

Barney attended the one-room Behnke School, along with thirty-five other first-to-eighth graders, for three years (1904–1907), until the demands of sustaining the family farm forced him to assist with the daily chores. In adult life he was frequently embarrassed by his lack of formal education, but he lived to see his children pursue educational opportunities that were not available to him.

The death of his father when Barney was five placed a heavy burden on his mother, who thereafter depended greatly on his older siblings to help raise the younger children. Availability of richer farm land immediately to the west of their present homestead prompted his mother, an astute manager, to continue acquiring acreage, eventually owning 480 acres of potentially tillable land in southern Marinette and Northern Oconto counties.

Clearing the newly purchased land extracted a heavy physical toll on the males in the Seefeldt family. Ability to guide a team of horses to pull the equipment necessary for clearing the land and cultivating the soil became a requisite skill-one inherited from their father, who amassed a small fortune by breeding and training draft horses at a time when the demand for the valuable animals far exceeded their availability. Barney learned at a young age that he had an affinity for horses and soon became an expert at getting his teams to perform difficult maneuvers-a skill that eventually served him well as a lumberjack during the process of loading the huge logs on sleds for transport to saw mills.

Barney left home at the age of fourteen to work as an apprentice carpenter for his neighbor and surrogate father, Gottlieb Gannigan, a builder of houses, barns, and storage sheds, using an ancient German technique of wooden pegs instead of nails to affix the structures of buildings. Gannigan's fame had spread throughout Northern Wisconsin during the 1900–1920's era of tornados, when buildings by Gannigan successfully withstood the horizontal forces of winds, while those built with nails collapsed from the swirling, sideward pressures.

As a carpenter, Barney's climbing ability soon earned him the title of spitzemann, meaning "man at the peak," a task assigned to one who joined the rafters at the peaks of roofs as the wooden structures were thrust skyward by a crew from opposite sides of the building. Armed with a bag of pegs and a mallet, Barney was able to fasten the rafters as fast as the men on the ground could hoist them into position. Thus, early in life Barney exhibited a fearlessness that impressed and frightened many of his coworkers.

When Wisconsin's cold winters interrupted the building of barns and sheds, Barney, under the tutelage of his brother Charlie, eight years his senior, joined the lumberjacks who populated the numerous lumber camps that operated in Northern Wisconsin and upper Michigan. His skill with a two-bladed ax and the stamina as part of a two-man sawing team earned him the reputation of a tireless worker who could produce more board feet of raw timber per day than could any of his contemporaries.

Barney's love for the outdoors developed early in life, when hunting and fishing routinely supplemented the table fare of pioneering families. Ducks, geese, rabbits, partridge, and deer were plentiful in the woods and meadows surrounding the homesteads. Early season runs of suckers, pike, smelt, herring, and carp provided variety to the protein-rich, fat-laden diets of pork and beef that were the mainstay of rural American families. Barney's prowess as a hunter and angler was well known in northeastern Wisconsin, especially when it was time to hunt down the wolves and coyotes that preyed on the local livestock. This love of all things wild and natural prepared Barney for his adventures in British Columbia, which are reported in the following thirteen chapters.

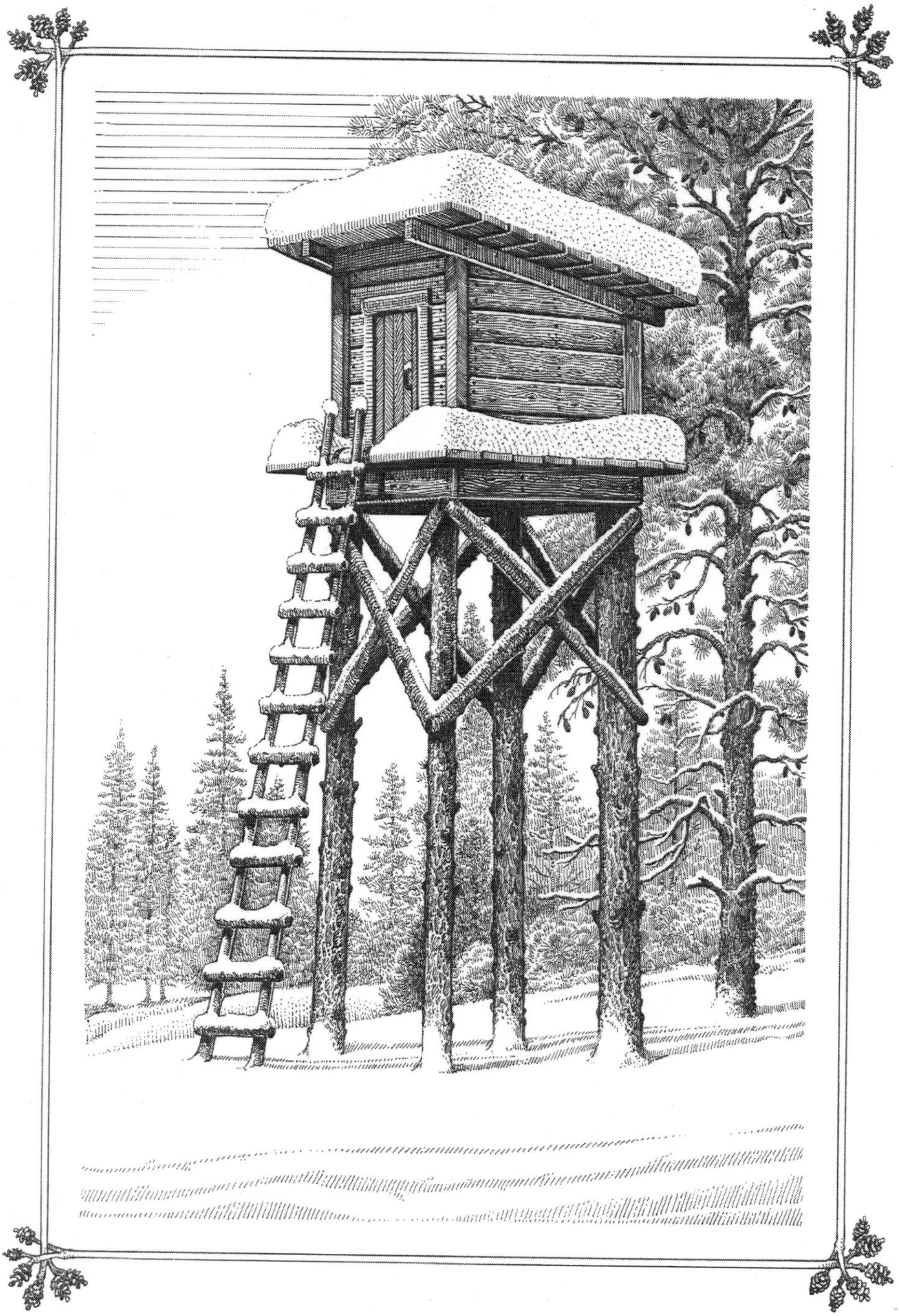

Chapter 1

In Quest of a New Lifestyle

Through his dust-stained goggles, Barney saw the silhouette of buildings against the red glow of the August sunset. "That has got to be Fargo," he muttered beneath the roar of his motorcycle, moving too fast for the conditions provided by the gravel roads over which he had traveled since leaving Minneapolis at sunrise that morning. In a telephone conversation earlier in the week he had promised a farmer named Lorenz that he would meet him at "the only restaurant in town, on main street," according to Lorenz. The job for which Barney had traveled from Appleton, Wisconsin, in such haste involved being a "teamster," meaning that the employee was to drive teams of horses, pulling a grain binder, for the purpose of harvesting part of North Dakota's vast wheat crop.

Barney had applied for the teamster's job as a matter of convenience because his final destination was British Columbia, where he hoped to homestead in its vast wilderness area. Although the Canadian Dominion Land Act was patterned after the United States Homestead Act of 1862, it was not as generous in its allocation of acres. Both acts were designed to attract permanent settlers who would improve the land, primarily as farmers.

Barney's goal was to earn sufficient money as a trapper so that he could return to his native Wisconsin and purchase a farm. Years of working as a carpenter during the spring and summer months and as a lumberjack and shipbuilder during the fall and winter had convinced him that money from hourly wages would not allow him to reach his objective. At age twenty-eight, he was ready to try an alternative way of earning his fortune.

Barney, ever a stickler for being on time, had driven his motorcycle, with attached sidecar, at reckless speeds throughout the day in order to meet his scheduled 8:00 p.m. appointment. Unable to find a map with an accurate estimate of the mileage involved, he had underestimated the time it would take him to travel from Appleton, Wisconsin, to Fargo, North Dakota. He reasoned that he could always travel late into the night if he was behind his projected schedule, but a steady rain throughout Wisconsin the previous day had slowed his travel on the slick, water-soaked gravel roads.

The reckless speeds at which Barney drove on the unpaved roads were reminiscent of his previous behavior. In 1918, as a twenty-year-old carpenter, he had attempted a ride in similar rainy conditions on his way to Marinette, Wisconsin, in preparation for reporting to the induction center for enlistment in the United States Army. In Appleton, Wisconsin, on a rainy night, he had missed the warning signal of an approaching freight train. The train's cowcatcher caught his motorcycle's sidecar, flipping Barney and the bike completely over the road into the opposite ditch. Fortunately for Barney, a motorist on the opposite side of the road had seen the accident and transported the unconscious cyclist to the area hospital. The diagnosis of a concussion, six broken ribs and a broken arm had delayed his induction into the armed forces until an armistice between the warring nations was signed in November 1918, negating his need for military service.

Knowing he was late, Barney had stopped at noon in Sauk Center, Minnesota, to buy a hamburger, which he ate with his free hand, while steering his cycle with the other. Now he was hungry and needed a shower to remove the layer of dust that covered him from head to toe. He could feel the caked mud that had spattered portions of his face where it was unprotected by his goggles. He realized that if farmer Lorenz was on time, he would not have a chance to clear the dust from his clothes and wash up before meeting him.

Barney reduced his speed when he reached the city limits, and soon was rewarded with a sign that stated **_Fargo, Population 2,500_**. As he drove down what appeared to be Fargo's only street he noted that all the businesses except two appeared to be closed for the day. The first building with lights was a grocery/general store and the second one advertised hamburgers and steaks.

"This must be the place," thought Barney, as he wheeled his motorcycle off the street. The cycle's progress was stopped by a raised platform of wooden planks that served as a sidewalk. Dismounting, he removed his goggles, reached for the bill of his cap, and swished it against his thigh, thereby expelling a cloud of dust from the cap and pants. Repeated slapping of the cap against his pants and shirt removed much of the day's accumulation of dust. When he thought himself presentable, Barney stepped on the sidewalk, climbed the three steps that placed him in front of the restaurant's heavy door, and peered into the lighted room.

Barney's entrance was greeted by stares from all occupants. Men dressed in denim shirts and overalls sat in groups of threes and fours at tables, eating their evening meals. Barney surmised that he had entered a closed society, a place where farmers met at the end of the day to discuss issues common to all of them. Any stranger who entered the room was apt to be thoroughly scrutinized as an intruder-a treatment the occupants were now imposing on Barney.

"Howdy, stranger," boomed a voice from behind the counter. "What brings you here and what can I do for you?" Barney presumed that the voice belonged to the proprietor.

"I'm here to meet Farmer Lorenz," stated Barney, feeling ill at ease and keenly aware that every ear was tuned for his reply.

"I'm John Lorenz," stated a tall, raw-boned man of about fifty years of age, as he arose from a table on the far side of the room. "You must be Safelt."

"Yes, I'm Barney Seefeldt," corrected Barney, as he strode forward to meet Lorenz.

"You said you can drive horses?" questioned Lorenz, abruptly.

"I've been driving horses since I was twelve," answered Barney, impressed by the direct manner of Lorenz. "I've driven teams of four horses, hauling logs on icy, hilly roads without any trouble," continued Barney, hoping that his brief explanation of driving skill and experience would sufficiently impress Lorenz and extract a job offer.

"Well, you don't need to worry about ice or hills here, but the job includes driving eight horses and keeping them pulling in a straight line for ten-hour days. Do you think you can handle that?" countered Lorenz.

Barney was aware that all eyes and ears were still tuned to the conversation between Lorenz and he. "Yes, I think I can," replied Barney with a voice that belied his confidence at the moment. "Give me a chance, and I'll show you what I can do."

Barney's direct manner seemed to please Lorenz because he replied, "All right, be at my farm at eight tomorrow morning for hitch-up. The job pays eight dollars a day and includes three meals and lodging. It lasts until all the wheat is cut, which I think will take two weeks. After tomorrow, we'll leave the binders in the field, but for now they are all parked at my place. Do you have a place to stay tonight?"

Without waiting for Barney's reply, he continued, "There's room in the bunkhouse. You're welcome to find a vacant bunk. There should be one left because there are already six men and my foreman sleeping there tonight. Get a bite to eat and then you can follow me home, and I'll see that you get set up for tomorrow morning." With that Lorenz returned to his table, leaving Barney to fend for himself. As Barney approached the counter to order his evening meal, he noted that although most of the men resumed their meals, they kept watching him and continued to do so while he ate.

Lorenz must have been watching him, too, because as soon as Barney had devoured his last bite, Lorenz arose and approached him. "Ready to go?" he stated, more as a command than a question.

"I'm ready," replied Barney. "I'll stay a ways behind you to keep out of the dust."

"Good thinking," replied Lorenz. "Its only three miles to my place, but you're right. The roads are plenty dusty because we haven't had rain in Fargo since early July."

Lorenz climbed into a 1924 Chevrolet pickup, backed it into Fargo's main street, and turned to the west. Barney had no difficulty following the trail of dust that soon hid the truck. For several miles the one-lane road ran parallel to continuous fields of wheat. The road then turned south and within a quarter mile the truck stopped in front of what Barney presumed to be Lorenz's farm. Barney noted that the expansive white house, sprawling red barn, and numerous metal grain storage sheds were all freshly painted and in good repair. On the far side of the yard stood a low-roofed rambling shed that apparently was home to the sixty-plus horses that were needed to pull the eight binders. Between the house and the barn stood a one-story log cabin that Barney presumed to be the bunk house Lorenz had mentioned earlier.

"Come on. I'll introduce you to the men. Bring your gear," commanded Lorenz as Barney pulled up next to his truck.

The cool August air had driven the teamsters into the bunkhouse, where Barney saw six men, engrossed in a card game, gathered around a low table in the center of the room. When Lorenz opened the door the men ceased their game and rose to see what caused their employer to enter their domain so late in the day.

"This is the man who completes our teamsters group," said Lorenz by way of introducing Barney. "Barney Safelt, from Wisconsin. Show him the empty bunk, Coleman, and make him feel at home." With that Lorenz turned and strode from the bunkhouse.

"Howdy," greeted the card player to whom Lorenz had directed his remark. "I'm John Coleman, foreman of this crew. The empty bunk is the top one behind you. You can store your stuff in the corner and hang your coat on the rack near the door. We're having a game of poker. Join if you like. By the way, these men are Jim, Elmer, Frank, Mark, Charlie, and Louie." Each man stepped forward to shake Barney's hand as he was introduced.

"Thanks, but I've been riding since six this morning. I'll wash up at the sink and hit the rack, if that's OK," said Barney.

"Suit yourself," replied Coleman, as he and the other teamsters returned to their seats, eager to resume their game. Barney, meanwhile, moved to the sink, splashed some cold water on his face, supplied by a hand pump that stood in the corner. He unrolled his sleeping bag, tossed it up to the bunk, undressed, and within minutes was fast asleep.

Barney was too tired to accept Coleman's invitation and equally wary of gambling with strangers. Years of living in lumber camps had taught him that friendships had to be earned. Expatriated from his home at age fourteen, he had become the protégé of his older brother, Charlie, who had taught him the rough-and-tumble life of a lumberjack. Initially, a spectator in the barroom brawls that served as Saturday evening entertainment in the lumbering towns in northern Wisconsin, Barney had soon become known as a skillful fighter in the fisticuffs that involved his burly brother. Known to have a prickly temper, Barney was anxious to avoid any trouble on his new job.

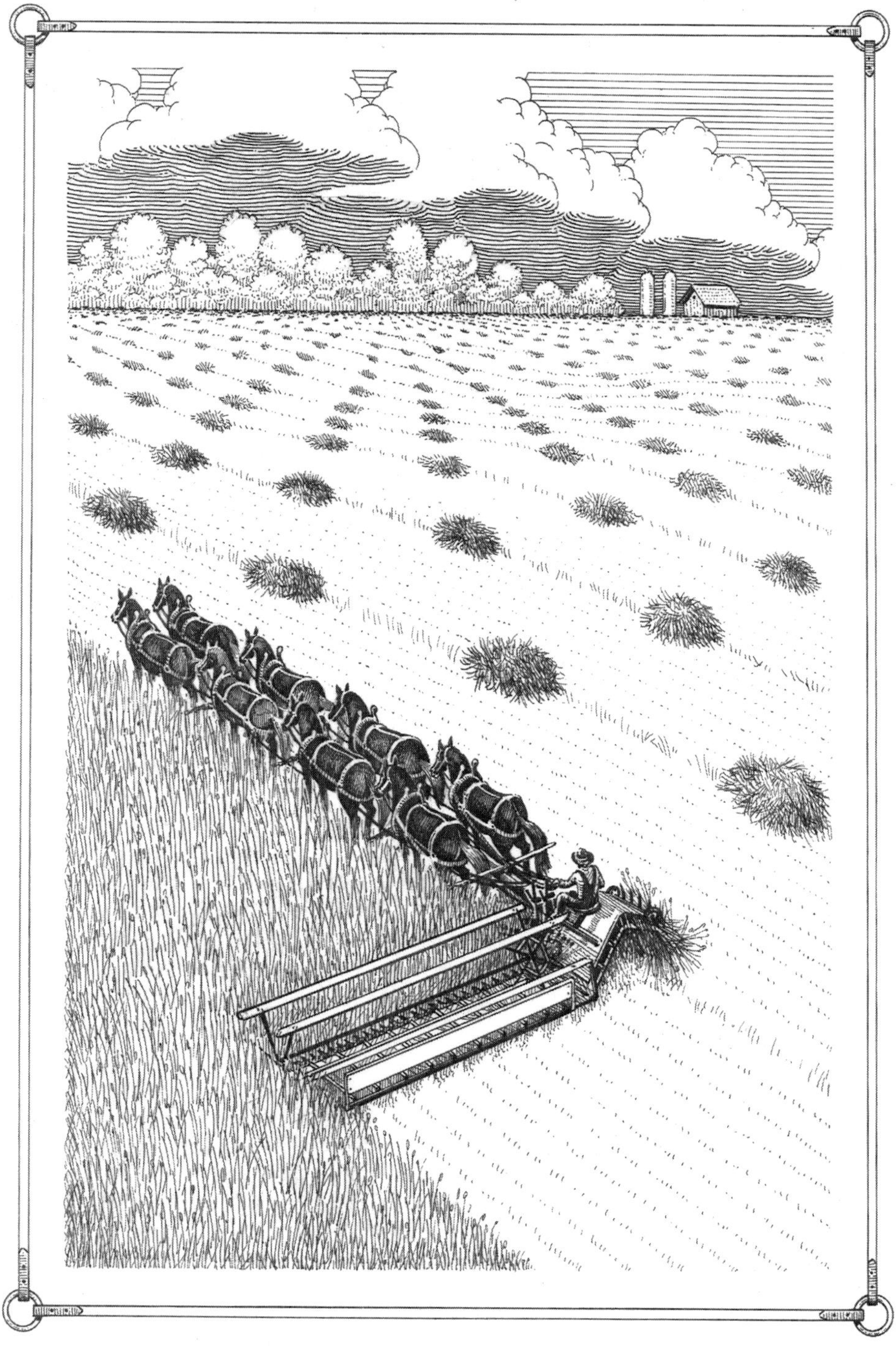

Chapter 2

A Questionable Partnership in North Dakota's Wheat Fields

"Roll out," boomed Coleman's voice. "Breakfast in five minutes."

To Barney, the call seemed to come within minutes after he went to sleep, but a look at his watch confirmed that it was 5:00 a.m.

"Why are we getting up at five o'clock?" asked Barney. "We can't cut wheat until the sun dries off the dew."

"You're in North Dakota now," counseled Coleman. "We don't have dew here, so we can start cutting as soon as we can get the horses harnessed and hitched. Now let's go to breakfast. It's a long day, and you'll need all the strength you can get before the day is over."

Barney resented the paternalistic tone of Coleman's remark, but instead of replying he nodded and followed the men to the porch of the farmhouse where Mrs. Lorenz and her assistant were serving a steaming hot breakfast of eggs, potatoes, ham, bacon, and coffee. Little did Coleman know that the invitation to breakfast would be the last cordial conversation between he and Barney before the events of the day impelled them toward a confrontation that would forever end Coleman's status as foreman.

Harnessing the sixty-four horses that constituted the eight hitches went without incident. However, Barney was appalled at the condition of the horses that were paraded out of the stable as each team was fitted with harnesses. As he viewed the horses, he estimated that nearly a third of them would not be able to pull the heavy binders for an entire day. In addition, many looked old and slow. All of the horses appeared to have been at pasture since last summer, as indicated by the layer of fat beneath their glossy coats.

Once all the horses had been assembled into teams of eight, foreman Coleman assigned each teamster and his hitch to a binder. Barney was assigned to the fifth binder, meaning that he would be cutting the fifth swath of wheat. Behind him, with his team of eight horses, was the driver whose name he remembered as "Louie." As expected, foreman Coleman hitched his team to the first binder and led the convoy down the road where they soon entered Lorenz's two-thousand-acre field of wheat.

"We expect to be halfway around the field by noon. We'll stop for lunch and rest the horses," announced Coleman. With a crack of his long blacksnake whip, he sent his eight horses into the field of waving wheat. Each of the teamsters followed in turn and by seven fifteen each of the binders was removing a sixteen-foot swath of the golden grain, which was mechanically tied into bundles and deposited behind the binders, later to be placed into stacks for retrieval by wagons that would transport the grain to the threshing machine parked at the entrance of the field.

By 10:00 a.m., as the temperature reached eighty degrees, Barney's apprehension about the condition of the horses became reality. He and the other teamsters had been forced to stop numerous times because the teams ahead of them were too exhausted to continue. Instead of resting the horses every hour as planned, the rest periods occurred every twenty minutes. During one of the frequent breaks Barney was approached by Louie, who was equally disgusted with the pace of the harvest.

"At this rate we'll never get halfway around this field by noon," suggested Louie.

"That was pretty clear by looking at the horses," replied Barney, feeling a kinship with the tall, blond fellow who seemed to feel as Barney did about the lack of progress. "If we are going to get anything done we will have to change the way the teams are hitched up. There are about forty good horses here, but the way Coleman has them hitched together slows down each binder."

"Well, it looks like we're moving again," noted Louie, seemingly anxious about anymore negative conversation as the long row of binders began to slowly crawl around the huge field. He and Barney mounted their machines, only to have the periodic rest periods continue throughout the morning. By noon the teamsters who were driving hitches five through eight were thoroughly disgusted with the inordinate time they had spent waiting for the teams ahead of them to recover sufficient energy to move forward.

"Whoa! We'll stop here for lunch," stated Coleman from his perch on the first binder.

The expressions on the faces of the teamsters as they pulled close to Coleman's binder told of their exasperation. Instead of completing one-half a lap, they had stopped when they were barely one-third of the way around the course.

"Unhitch your horses and drive them into a circle over here," gestured Coleman, indicating a spot where the grain had been cut. "Feed and water should arrive in a few minutes. Stake your teams apart far enough so they don't steal each other's feed."

As Coleman spoke, Lorenz and his hired hands arrived with wagons carrying hay and water. As the thirsty animals sucked up the refreshing water, Barney's earlier impression of the poor condition of the tired beasts was reinforced. When hay was distributed, the animals seemed too tired to move forward for their noon meal. Barney had been raised around working horses, and what he saw made him angry. He blamed farmer Lorenz for the poor condition of the animals, but he was also incensed with the way the teams had been matched up by Coleman. As he strode to the place where the noon meal was being served he could barely contain his indignation.

"Well, we didn't even get halfway around the field." he retorted as he approached Coleman. "Most of those horses are not in a shape to work six more hours. I think we should reassemble the teams so that the best horses are in the front hitches and not hold everyone up." Barney was aware that his comments directly criticized Coleman and that the criticism had been overheard by all the teamsters, but he was so disgusted with the morning's experience that he did not care about Coleman's feelings. He had determined that if the situation could not be changed, he was ready to quit immediately.

"You trying to tell me how to run this outfit?" inquired an angry Coleman, who no doubt was also disappointed with the progress made that morning.

"Someone has to tell you how to run it because it is plain that you don't know enough to run it right," shot back Barney, his quick temper near a boiling point.

Coleman's face turned red. He raised his left elbow and drew back his right hand as if to strike Barney. Before he could deliver his blow Barney detected a movement behind him, a fist shot out and Coleman was lying on the ground holding his jaw. In a flash teamster Louie was standing over Coleman, waiting to resume the fight. Coleman, however, was so taken by surprise by the blow that he did not even attempt to get up.

"What's going on here?" commanded Lorenz, who had approached the group just as the encounter between Coleman and Barney began.

"This man doesn't know crap about horses or how to get this wheat cut," answered Barney, who now realized that it was Louie who had stepped forward to "coldcock" Coleman, anticipating a similar attempt that Barney would have had to make a brief second later. "If you want to get this wheat cut, you'll have to change the way the horses are hitched. Most of the horses are not in shape to work ten hours a day. They are not ready to work now, and they won't be able to work if you only feed them hay."

Lorenz had seen the sweaty coats of the horses and the lack of progress by the teamsters, so he was aware that changes were in order. Seeing his foreman on the ground, without any support from the other teamsters convinced him that the operation was in trouble. "What do you suggest?" he asked.

"Let me pick the horses for the eight hitches," replied Barney. "If we change teams, some of us will be able to make it around the field by evening. These horses need oats-five pounds of ground oats for each horse three times a day. They can't work like this on hay alone. If we keep frogging along like we did this morning, it will take three weeks instead of two, and even then we may not have this wheat cut."

Lorenz saw that his foreman had picked himself off the ground, but he appeared dazed and in no condition to resume his foreman's role. Lorenz surmised that Coleman would not be able to control the teamsters from this point on. The faces of the other teamsters were filled with expectation regarding his next move. He realized that he must move decisively or risk having a mutiny on his hands.

Lorenz's analysis of the situation had begun when he entered the field and observed that the teams were far from their expected destination. The lathered coats of the horses told him that his timetable for cutting his wheat would require modification.

"OK, Safelt. You pick the teams for the hitches this afternoon." And looking at Coleman, said, "John, you come with me. We'll go to town for grain and supplies. Safelt, use seven hitches this afternoon."

Motioning his foreman to follow him, Lorenz strode to his wagon, with Coleman, still rubbing his bruised jaw, in tow. With a slap of the reins, he drove his team and wagon from the field, leaving the teamsters with the assumption that Barney was in charge of the afternoon's schedule.

Barney wasted no time in taking command of the situation. "OK, men. See that your teams get enough water and hay, then go to the tent and get some food. We'll take an hour to rest the horses. At one fifteen we'll rearrange the teams for this afternoon. I will take the lead team. Louie will follow me. Hitches seven and eight from this morning will be three and four this afternoon. Hitches two, three, and four of this morning will be five, six, and seven this afternoon. Let's see how that works. We may need to make some more changes after today." The last statement was made to keep the men on their toes, and also to alert them that he intended to be in charge after today.

With Barney leading the convoy of binders, the teamsters began the afternoon with a sense of determination that had been lacking in the morning. Each teamster knew that he was being evaluated by Barney because they saw him turning frequently in his seat to see which teams were not keeping up with the group. Midway through the afternoon he instructed hitches six and seven to trade places, but from then on the teams moved forward in unison. By evening all the teams had completed the full cycle, although the last three hitches did not complete their rotation until the first four units had exited the field.

Supper, as Lorenz called the evening meal, was unusually quiet. The men had been subjected to a day of physical labor during which their hands and arms had endured the stress of manipulating multiple reins, while at the same time trying to have their teams keep pace with the row of binders ahead of them. They were physically exhausted, but most likely the silence was due to the emotional stress of not knowing what lay before them in the days ahead. At noon they had witnessed the removal of their foreman, replaced by a stranger about whom neither they nor Lorenz knew anything except that he was not afraid to speak up and that he acted as though he could back up what he said.

Their new boss, Barney, seemed to have an uncanny ability to judge the pulling abilities of horses. Teams that Barney had assembled at noon performed miracles compared with the combinations that had been pulling the binders that morning. The fact that by evening even the slowest of the hitches had completed one lap of the giant field was a feat that even the most optimistic among them would have doubted at noon.

That evening, under Barney's orders, the horses were rubbed down with gunny sacks, curried, and combed prior to being led to water and fed. The oats that Barney had prescribed were on hand, eagerly devoured by the horses before consuming the alfalfa hay that was available in baled form. Through Barney's example, the teamsters learned that their first duty each day was to take care of their horses.

The somber mood of the men continued during and after supper. As they entered the bunkhouse there was no jovial anticipation of the nightly poker game. Each man sat silently on the edge of this bunk, not knowing what the next few hours would bring. The lower bunk nearest the door, occupied last night by foreman Coleman, was conspicuously empty. His presence had also been missed at supper, but Lorenz had not mentioned his name, nor did anyone feel sufficiently bold to inquire about him. Wisely, Lorenz had made arrangements for Coleman to assist a neighboring farmer with his harvest, thereby sparing his foreman the indignity of sharing the bunkhouse with Barney and Louie and thus preventing further encounters. Unfortunately, the precautions arranged by Lorenz applied only to the harvest. The free time of the combatants was out of Lorenz's control as he would learn the following Monday.

As Barney entered the bunkhouse that evening he could not escape the tension in the room. He was also keenly aware that Louie and he had caused it. The men stared at the floor after acknowledging that he had entered room. Experience had taught Barney that bitterness and distrust among workers only led to more trouble. In his role of foreman-by-accident, he sensed a responsibility to restore harmony and fellowship among the teamsters. He realized that he could talk to the men in an attempt to explain his version of the confrontation with Coleman, but a sixth sense told him that many of the men already agreed with his actions. Their awkward silence was merely an indication that they did not know what else to expect from him.

Instead of attempting to ease the tension with conversation, Barney resorted to a technique that his experiences in numerous lumber camps had taught him. Music was an ideal way to break the tension and to relieve the stress of a day's work. He resorted to what he had done so often in similar situations-he brought out his button accordion from the sidecar of his motorcycle and began to play dance tunes that had been favorites during World War I. Almost immediately, Barney sensed that the tension was beginning to disappear. To Barney's delight, Louie reached under his bunk and brought out a large, black case, which contained a concertina. Louie, it turned out, was an accomplished musician. As Barney and Louie combined their talents, they realized that they had basically the same repertoire, or perhaps more correctly, Louie could play any tune that Barney introduced. Soon the other teamsters began to hum and sing the lyrics of the popular songs.

After an hour of playing, which completely exhausted Barney's list of songs, the musicians stored their instruments, complete with the knowledge that music and song had united the men in a way that would have been unpredictable several hours earlier. That evening the men slept with the impression that their future as teamsters would be less stressful than the day they had just completed.

Cutting the giant field of wheat soon turned into a routine set of chores that the crew readily accepted. The men knew what to expect in Barney's regimented day. They could see the acres of wheat disappear behind the steadily moving binders. Farmer Lorenz was outspoken in his praise of the men and their progress whenever they broke for meals.

As foreman, Barney consulted frequently with Lorenz, but he kept his distance from the men except to direct their actions each morning, noon, and evening. His only exception to the self-imposed isolation from the men was his growing affection for the young, raw-boned titan named Louie, who had so conveniently relieved Barney of the need to fight Coleman. Barney was impressed at the way Louie handled his eight-horse hitch, at his ability to do more than his share of the work, and by his willingness to assist the less capable men with their chores. But most of all Barney admired Louie's musical talent.

Louie had the amazing ability to play "by ear," a characteristic both men shared. Neither man could read music, but hearing a tune immediately made it theirs. Louie possessed a beautiful baritone voice, which he used to sing or hum tunes throughout the day. His clear, distinct whistle tunes entertained the teamsters who were downwind from his second position in the convoy. In his happy, gently way, Louie ingratiated himself to the other teamsters, who wondered if this could be the same person who had so forcefully dispatched their foreman several days ago. The gentle giant that had such a tender touch on the reins of his teams seemed totally different from the man who had sent Coleman to the ground with one swift blow of his fist.

As the men were sitting around a campfire on their fifth day of harvest, their songfest was interrupted by the headlights of a vehicle entering the driveway. Abruptly, Louie stopped playing and retreated to the bunkhouse. Barney was surprised by Louie's sudden exit, but he said nothing. Louie's hasty departure was not lost on the other teamsters, who also exchanged quizzical glances. What was there about the car that had such a profound affect on Louie? No one dared to ask, but the event stayed in Barney's memory as the events of the next several months unfolded.

Several men climbed out of the car and entered Lorenz's house. The confident way in which they strode suggested to Barney that they knew Lorenz and were not strangers on his premises. Within minutes the men, accompanied by Lorenz, came to the campfire.

"Barney, these men are from Fargo. They have heard of your playing, and they want to know if you and Louie will play for a dance that they intend to hold tomorrow night at the city hall?"

"That depends," said Barney.

"We'll pay fifteen dollars each if you play from nine to one." Barney was immediately interested because the fee was nearly twice his daily wage.

"How big is the hall? How many people do you expect will be there?"

"The hall holds about three hundred people, but about one hundred couples can dance at one time. We need waltzes and polkas, and we'll have Jesse Schwartz there to call square dances. Do you think you can handle that?"

"With a hall that size, we'll need a loudspeaker and another man for the band—someone who can play drums. If you can get those two, you have a deal," said Barney. He knew from his experience of having played at numerous weddings for friends in Grover, Wisconsin, that such a large group would challenge the volume of a concertina and accordion. A set of drums, amplified by a microphone, would guarantee that the beat could be heard by the dancers even if the tune was barely audible.

Barney had not consulted Louie about playing for the dancers, but he was confident that Louie would accept. However, Louie seemed strangely hesitant when told of the arrangements that Barney had made. With some additional persuasion, most likely by the thought of earning some easy money, he finally agreed to be part of the orchestra.

"Why was the outgoing Louie, with his great ability to play any tune the dancers requested, so reluctant to play in public?" questioned Barney to himself. He did not know Louie sufficiently well to ask about his unwillingness to play, but reasoned that Louie must have had some disappointing experiences with public performances in the past. Nevertheless, the evening of the dance approached without anymore conversation about Louie's reluctance to participate or how the musicians would function. Barney reasoned that with Louie's musical talent the evening would be a success. According to one of the local teamsters, a drummer had been hired by the committee, so Barney approached the evening with his usual air of self-assurance, confident that the band would perform successfully.

As Barney and Louie rode their cycles to the town hall's parking lot at eight thirty they were surprised to see that a large crowd had already gathered. Men in their shirt sleeves and women in their Sunday best were conversing in small groups, enjoying the refreshing breeze prior to entering the sweltering hot dance hall, in which the windows had been opened just minutes before the musicians arrived. Barney surmised there were very few strangers in the crowd, judging by the handshaking, hugs, and greetings that occurred as the arriving folks greeted one another.

Whether because of deprivation or because they enjoyed good music, the crowd responded enthusiastically to each set, whether waltz or polka. The dance floor was filled with sweating bodies who seemed to enjoy whatever the musicians played. Ovations followed each set, encouraging the musicians to play an additional number.

Following the eleven o'clock intermission, Barney whispered to Louie, "Can you play the next set without me? I'm going to ask that pretty girl in the yellow dress to dance with me." Barney and all of the young men had kept their eyes glued on a beautiful girl who danced with numerous men, but who returned to sit with two middle-aged people, most likely her parents, after each dance. She did not accompany any of the men to the popular bar, nor did she go outside after dancing, as did many of her young counterparts.

"Fine," replied Louie. "She's with her ole man, who is bigger than you are, so be careful. I talked to some of the local boys during intermission. Her dad is the biggest land owner in this county, but I don't think he's looking for a son-in-law. I think John Coleman has his eye on her, too. He has danced with her several times."

"I'm only going to dance with her," responded Barney. Before Louie could add to the conversation, Barney was off to ask for his dance.

As Louie's concertina broke into strands of a popular waltz Barney and his partner glided across the dance floor, joined by dozens of others. Barney had noted that the girl skillfully followed her partner, regardless of the partner's dancing ability. Barney, who considered himself an accomplished dancer, was able to verify that his young partner floated like a butterfly. No wonder every eye had been on her. She had the ability to make her partners look graceful, despite their shortcomings.

As Barney and his partner were midway through Louie's second waltz, Barney was nearly knocked off his feet by a solid blow to his back. Thinking that the collision had been caused by someone who was drunk, Barney regained his step and looked to see who had caused the problem. "Why don't you look where you're going? Do you have two left feet?" inquired a belligerent Coleman, who had delivered the blow and now had guided his partner next to Barney.

Angry at seeing his old nemesis, and disgusted at having his dance interrupted, Barney replied, "Let's step outside, and I'll show you what my left feet can do."

Coleman cocked his head toward the door in agreement as both men walked their partners off the dance floor. When they entered the parking lot, Barney realized that he had walked into a trap. Coleman stopped near the parked cars and turned to face Barney. As he did so, he was joined by four men who formed a semicircle around Barney. Unable to extract himself, Barney made the best of a bad situation. Before Coleman had time to react, Barney slapped him hard with his left hand. As Coleman's head moved to the right from the force of the cuff, Barney's right fist landed a crushing blow to his jaw, sending Coleman to the ground.

As Barney dispatched Coleman, one of Coleman's henchmen jumped on Barney's back, pinning his arms to his sides. In his semi—helpless position, Barney dodged a blow to his face from the thug immediately in front of him, but the punch caught him squarely on his nose, causing blood to squirt down his white shirt. Barney's mind was preparing his

body to take the imminent beating when the man on his back was forcefully removed.

"I thought you might need a hand." Louie grinned and subdued the rider with a vicious kick to the abdomen and a solid right hand to the jaw as the man staggered to his feet. Barney, in the meantime, had regained his balance and outraged to the point of delirium, confronted the third assailant and pummeled him to helplessness. The fourth assailant, surmising that these two teamsters were not ordinary pugilists, melted into the crowd before Barney and Louie had an opportunity to catch him.

"OK. The fight is over. Free drinks at the bar for everyone. Let's get back to the dance floor," announced the chairman of the organizing committee, eager to restore order and to continue what had been to that point, a thoroughly enjoyable evening.

"Not for us. You can celebrate all you want, but Louie and I are through for the night," replied Barney, who needed some cold water to take the sting out of his swollen nose.

As they recovered their instruments, amid appeals from the crowd that they continue to play, they were aware that Coleman and his group did not have many friends among the attendees. Coleman, however, proved to be a careful planner. When Barney pushed down the foot pedal to start his motorcycle he was greeted by silence. Coleman and his men had removed the cycle's spark plugs to ensure that Barney would not have transportation, regardless of how the fight ended. Seeing the plight of the musicians, a young man with a pickup truck offered to transport Barney and his cycle to Lorenz's home.

As Barney and Louie sat in the bunkhouse after their Saturday night outing, they reflected on the week's activities. Within six days they had been involved in two fights that they had neither planned nor anticipated. The fights occurred because the two teamsters had a zest for living and were not about to let obstacles get in their way. This forceful way of expressing their opinions had previously led to numerous physical encounters for both of them. Their preference for resolving conflicts physically would bring additional difficulties, but at this point in their lives neither was willing to change his reaction to physical challenges. The code by which they lived their daily lives left little room for compromise, especially if fighting provided an option.

"I hear you boys found trouble at the dance last night," greeted Lorenz, when Barney and Louie filed in for breakfast on Sunday morning.

"Trouble found us, but we didn't exactly run from it," offered Louie, understandably confident that he was equal to any physical challenge that came his way.

"Your foreman came to the dance, looking for a fight, but he picked on the wrong men," suggested Barney.

"So I'm told," replied Lorenz. "I think Coleman has learned his lesson. You will not have anymore trouble from him."

"We can't seem to avoid trouble here, so Louie and I are going to leave this afternoon," announced Barney, having briefly discussed their situation in the bunkhouse with Louie last evening. Sensing that Lorenz was disappointed with the constant fighting, they had decided to end their employment that morning.

"I can't afford to lose you two now, when the grain is already too ripe for cutting. I want you to reconsider, and to make it worth your while, I'll raise your pay to ten dollars a day, with a twenty dollar bonus for each of you if you stay until all the grain is cut."

Barney, sensing a genuine expression of need and gratitude from Lorenz, spoke for both of the men. "All right, we'll stay this week, but Saturday is our last day. If the work continues like it did these past four days, we'll have your wheat cut by then."

"It's a deal," announced Lorenz, happy that his crew would remain intact for the remainder of the harvest. "This is the best grain I've had in four years, and I don't want to leave it in the field. If it doesn't rain before we finish, I'll be able to recover somewhat from the years of drought that has wiped out many wheat farmers in North Dakota."

Earlier that Sunday morning as Barney and Louie washed their clothes, Louie approached Barney with a question that he apparently had been pondering for several days. "It's been fun working with you. What are you going to do when this job is done?" Barney interpreted this question from Louie as a need for companionship, sort of like a little brother asking an older brother for advice.

"I'm on my way to British Columbia when I finish here. I want to apply for a homestead and try to make some big money," replied Barney.

"What do you mean by homesteading? It sounds like farming to me."

"Not really. You go to the land office, make your application, and they assign some land to you. You build a cabin and improve the land and in three years you can have three hundred and twenty acres all of your own."

"How much money do you need for a homestead?" asked Louie.

"Only ten dollars for the land, and I'll need some money for tools and some building equipment, but I'm not going there to farm. I'm going there to trap furs and live off the land by hunting.

Furs are selling for premium prices in Canada, and I think I can make a good living as a trapper. I grew up in northern Wisconsin, where I hunted and trapped all my life. I'm good at it and it beats driving a team of horses for a living. I've been a carpenter, lumberjack, shipbuilder, and all-around-worker, but none of those jobs ever paid enough so I could buy a farm. That's why I want to make some big money fast, and trapping is the best way I know of to do it."

Louie's eyes began to sparkle as Barney spoke optimistically about the life of a trapper in British Columbia's wilderness. "I don't have anywhere to go after this job, so if you'll have me I'd like to be your partner," announced Louie, ever ready for a new adventure.

Barney had developed a genuine liking for the big blond teamster, but he was surprised by Louie's offer. Certainly, there would be advantages to having a partner in what Barney envisioned as a lonely four months, but Barney suspected that Louie's skills as a trapper may not be as refined as his own. In addition, having a partner would mean splitting whatever profits resulted from the venture. However, because of the many unknown aspects of life in the wilderness and Louie's ability to be present when trouble arose, Barney was favorably inclined to include Louie in his homesteading adventure. Never one to linger about decisions, Barney consented to take Louie along when he traveled to British Columbia.

Thus, on a Sunday afternoon in August of 1925, in Fargo, North Dakota, two relative strangers formed a partnership that propelled them into adventures that would try their endurance and leave one of them wondering about the fate of the other for the remainder of his life.

Lorenz, ever grateful that Barney and Louie had agreed to help him complete his harvest, offered to employ the men as permanent laborers on his farm. "Nope, we're off to British Columbia to become homesteaders and fur trappers," announced Louie, to Barney's chagrin.

"I know a little about homesteading in Canada, having considered that as an option if my wheat continues to drive me toward bankruptcy," said Lorenz. "Do you know where you want to homestead?"

"We're really interested in trapping, not farming," injected Barney, disappointed and irritated that Louie had announced their intentions to Lorenz. "We're going to British Columbia," he continued, not really sure of how they would get there, but eager to extract them from anymore conversation about the topic with Lorenz. However, Lorenz seemed genuinely interested in his teamsters' plans and continued the conversation.

"You'll need birth certificates and driver's licenses when you cross the border and when you file your claims," announced Lorenz, sensing that he was talking to two novices regarding the topic of homesteading. As Lorenz continued to explain the process of acquiring land in Canada to the teamsters, Barney became more interested, but Louie suddenly lost interest.

"What's wrong?" asked Barney, noting Louie's sudden withdrawal from the conversation.

"I don't have a birth certificate nor a driver's license," answered Louie. "My wallet and all my belongings were lost when our house burned."

"I can get you a driver's license in a few days, and I may even be able to get you a temporary birth certificate," offered Lorenz. "Come to Fargo with me tomorrow after we get done cutting. I know a judge there who owes me a few favors. If anyone can help us, he is the one." By now Lorenz was convinced that the man he had hired as Louie Harris, and the one who had been instrumental in keeping his crew of teamsters together, had something to hide in his background. However, Lorenz was not one to harshly judge someone who had done him a favor.

"OK, if you think you can swing it," said Louie, but clearly upset with the process of getting some official identification.

As Barney listened to the discussion, he was baffled by Louie's reaction. For the third time in a week, he had seen Louie resort to strange behavior when strangers were involved. Normally, the gregarious Louie loved to talk to people, but the thought of having to appear before a judge had terrorized him.

When the two men were alone in the bunkhouse, Louie approached Barney. "Will they take my fingerprints when I apply for a license?" he asked.

"No, I don't think so," explained Barney. "But what if they do? It doesn't hurt and the ink wears off in a day."

"I just don't want anyone having my fingerprints," explained Louie.

As the men finished their personal chores that Sunday afternoon, Barney's mind kept going over the anxiety expressed by Louie at the thought of being fingerprinted. What was it in Louie's past that caused fear over such a simple procedure? Then, too, there had been an unusual hesitation one evening when one of the teamsters asked Louie his last name. "Er, Harris" had been Louie's response, but Barney detected a lack of conviction in the answer, as though the name had been grasped as the first one that came to Louie's mind. Was Louie running from his past? Why had he been so concerned about the men who came to Lorenz's home to ask them to play at the dance? As these thoughts rumbled through Barney's mind he eventually resolved the problem by concluding that Louie's past was not any of his concern. Louie had been a steadfast friend and a timely defender. Barney decided that he would suppress any further questions about Louie's past. According to Barney's code of living, Louie had passed the test of suitability for partnership.

True to his word, Lorenz was able to convince the local judge that Louie's identification had been lost in a fire, and that there was not time to request duplicates from his self-reported home in Wyoming. If the judge sensed any irregularities in Louie's answers, he concealed his suspicions and moved ahead with the application. Most likely Louie's request was not the first time the old judge had been asked to assist a young man who seemed unwilling to reveal his past.

"You can pick up your driver's license on Friday afternoon. With any luck, your temporary birth certificate will be ready then, too," announced the judge as he looked at Louie over spectacles perched near the end of his nose. Louie's sigh of relief was not lost on Lorenz and the judge, but neither was about to interfere with the young man and his attempt to reestablish his identity. Whatever Louie's name had been before today, from now on he would be known as Louie Harris. He left the courthouse oblivious to the fact that Lorenz had used his best persuasive powers to convince the judge that for whatever reason, Louie needed another chance and this was the opportunity to grant it to him.

Lorenz, however, sensed that the teamsters may need additional help. "There is a little town near the Canadian border called Neche," he responded. "If you enter Canada there you will not run into any border patrols. It is right across from Gretna, on the Manitoba side and about one hundred and fifty miles from here. After that you will have about one hundred and ten miles to Winnipeg, which is the best place to catch a train. Sell your cycles in Winnipeg and ride the train. It will save time and you'll have a much better chance of getting rid of them in Winnipeg than in Prince Rupert, if that is where you're going."

Sunday morning found Barney and Louie outside the bunkhouse, saying farewell to their fellow teamsters. After finishing the field of wheat the previous noon, farmer Lorenz had treated the teamsters to a keg of beer and a beef barbeque to cap off a productive two weeks. Wages of each teamster were paid in cash, including generous bonuses to all the drivers. Beer flowed freely as Barney and Louie played and the teamsters sang and drank away the afternoon. By now word had spread that Barney and Louie were leaving the next day, so the festivities were clouded with the nostalgia that comes when all present know that friendships must end, with the unlikelihood of ever being renewed. Barney liked and respected the six workers, who in turn, had developed a true affection for their itinerant boss. Louie, who did not have to bear Barney's responsibility to the men, was a favorite among them and seemed reluctant to leave.

Sensing that leaving would become more difficult if they lingered, and becoming more concerned about Louie's hesitation to start his cycle, Barney pushed down the starter, adjusted his goggles, and started down the road to Winnipeg, by way of Fargo, knowing that Louie would follow. With sufficient cash in their pockets, and their worldly possessions with them, the ex-teamsters set off on the first leg of their journey to the Canadian wilderness.

Crossing the border into Canada proved to be uneventful, as Lorenz had suggested. He correctly noted that there was no checkpoint on the rural country intersection between the two countries, nor did the travelers encounter any officials on the Canadian side of the border. Thus, that evening as they motored into Winnipeg, the two dust-covered prospective homesteaders felt confident that they were capable of dealing with whatever obstacles came their way.

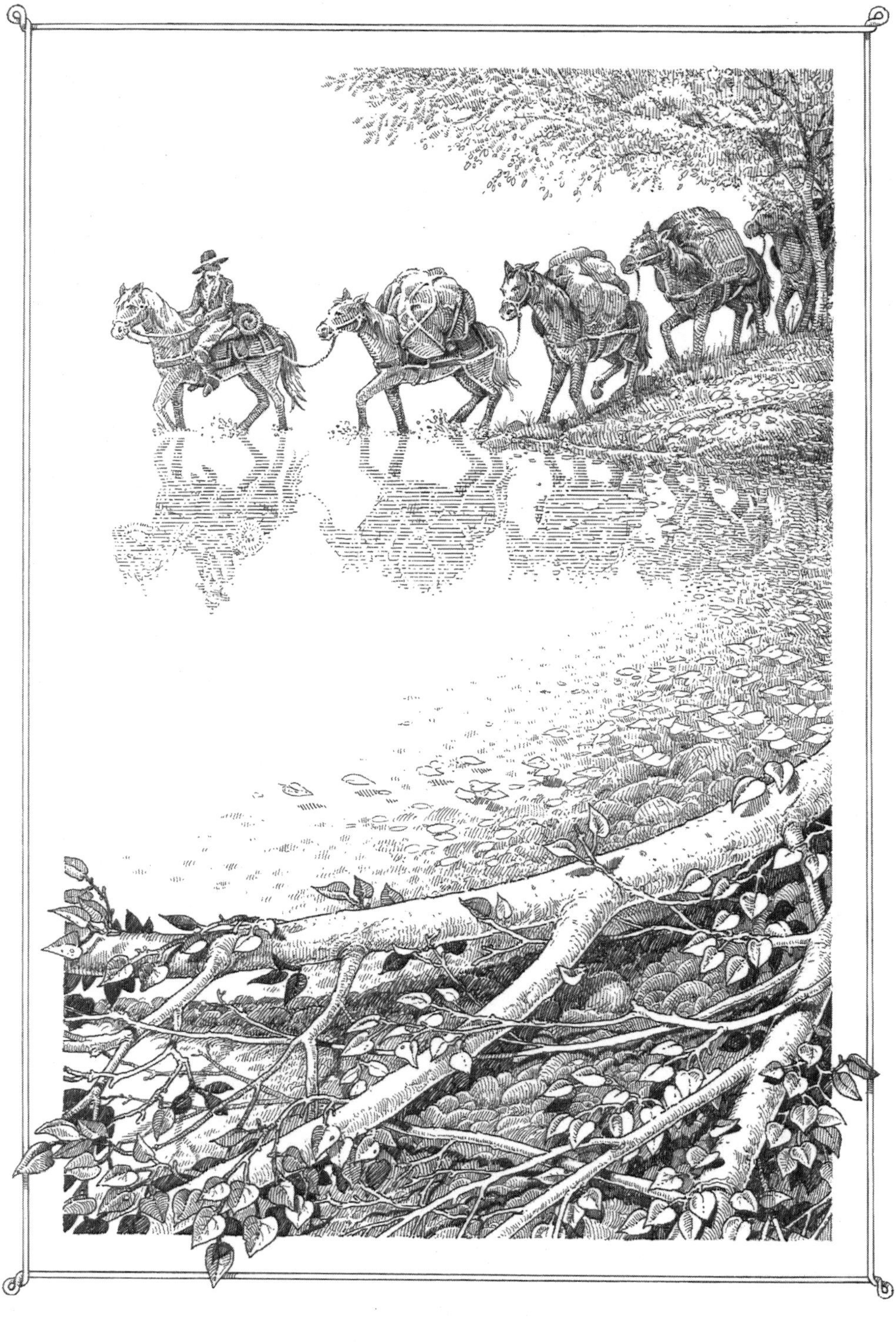

Chapter 3

To Winnipeg, Prince Rupert, and Hazelton

Winnipeg was bustling with activity as the two cyclists made their way through the south side residential section into the city's business district. Questions to local residents about the location of the rail depot soon found them at the busy center of the city. A large sign stated that the station was served by the Canadian National Railways, Grand Trunk Railway System, Central Vermont Railway. The potential homesteaders headed to the nearest booth with the intention of purchasing one-way tickets to Prince Rupert, British Columbia. Surprised and disappointed that the trip would take four days and that the train would possibly stop nearly a hundred times during its cross-country route before it reached Prince Rupert, Barney and Louie began to question farmer Lorenz's wisdom about taking the train instead of driving their cycles. After considering that they did not know the condition of the roads nor the types of weather they were likely to encounter in their two-thousand-and-five-hundred-mile journey, they resigned themselves to a restful, relaxing ride on the train. Both rationalized that travel by train would be safer than attempting to navigate the unknown distance by motorcycle. By train they would be dry and could travel by night-conditions that could not be guaranteed if they rode their cycles.

Reluctantly, the men sought directions to Winnipeg's cycle shop with the intention of selling their transportation. Both realized that autumn was not a good time to sell cycles, but their situation left them no alternative.

"Seventy-five dollar each" announced the owner of the combination garage/sporting goods store.

"They're worth a lot more than that,' exclaimed Barney, knowing that they had no real bargaining power.

"Suit yourself," announced the owner. "I won't be able to sell them this fall. If I'm lucky I may be able to get rid of them next spring."

"OK," announced Barney, "but you know you are getting a good deal. If we are back here in the spring, I hope we will be able to buy them for the same price." With that rather crusty exchange the two men accepted the owner's distasteful offer and returned to the train depot.

After purchasing "pullman tickets," ensuring that they would have a place to sleep for the next four nights, the prospective homesteaders set out to explore the accommodations of the Canadian National Railway. As the big locomotive pulled the combined passenger and freight train out of Winnipeg, Louie wandered from car to car, exchanging news and views with anyone who would engage him in conversation. Barney, in contrast, spent his time looking at the change of scenery as the train made its leisurely way across the lakes and woods of Manitoba into the flat, prairie fields of Saskatchewan and Alberta. Refreshing one-half day stops in the grain storage centers of Saskatoon and Edmonton gave the travelers an opportunity to stretch their legs in preparation for the last day of their journey.

As the train moved to the western edge of Alberta, entering the extensive Jasper National Park, the trappers got their first sight of the Rocky Mountains. Both had heard tales of the extensive fur trade that existed there almost one hundred years ago, but neither had any experience hunting or trapping in such rugged hills, steep valleys, and numerous lakes that constituted the landscape. As the train followed the river valleys on its way to Prince George, and hence to Prince Rupert the country seemed devoid of civilization except for the numerous hamlets within a stone's throw of the railway. Beyond the little towns there were no roads leading into the forests. The only signs of penetration into the cedars and hemlocks that lined both sides of the tracks for endless miles were the smaller rivers and streams that forcefully added their contributions to the mighty river as it flowed westward toward the Pacific Ocean.

If Barney and Louie were apprehensive about the suitability of British Columbia for their kind of homesteading, their fears were soon erased. The train took them through mile after mile of dense wilderness. Both had hunted in large, unmarked tracts of forest before, but the vastness of the view that was available to them from the elevated rails was overwhelming. Realizing that the immense wilderness to the north was without civilization except for bands of nomadic Indians, Barney and Louie were reminded that in several days they were to inhabit this land.

Late on the fourth day of their excursion from Winnipeg the travelers heard the conductor announce, "Prince Rupert. Take all your belongings. Train leaves here for Prince George at ten o'clock tomorrow morning." With duffle bags in hand, the two homesteaders searched the billboards for signs of a hotel. Rows of weather-beaten, wooden, one-story houses lined the streets surrounding the rail station. Several hundred feet beyond the depot the men spied some two-story buildings which seemed to indicate that the business section of the town was concentrated at the water's edge.

A sign **Prince Rupert Hotel and Bar** attracted the travelers' attention. They needed accommodations for several days while they purchased supplies and filed applications for their homesteads. They had no indication where their lands would be located, nor how they would get there. Youthful optimism suggested that if someone pointed them in the right direction, they would find whatever land was assigned to them. With this thought in mind, they walked into the hotel in search of lodging.

"Hello, strangers," boomed a voice from behind a bar of polished mahogany that lined the entire front of the building. "What can I do for you?"

"We need a room for three or four days," answered Barney. "We're here to file for a homestead and buy enough supplies to last us for several months while we trap for furs."

"I've got a room, but it's too late to file for land today. Government office opens at nine tomorrow morning. You'll find the federal courthouse, post office, and Royal Mounted Police office all in the same building. It's the three-story, white brick building on this street. It's the only brick building in town, so you can't miss it. Let me show you your room. How about supper? I run the only restaurant in town and my Mary sure can cook."

"Sounds like a good deal to us," suggested Barney, happy for the prospects of a solid bed and the opportunity to start their quest for a homestead the following morning. Barney surmised that the hotel owner, who introduced himself as Pat Shea, probably knew anything and everything the men would need to know concerning supplies and the process of homesteading. "We'll put our bags in the room and be down for supper," announced Barney, confident that their eager host would provide them with much-needed information at the earliest possible moment.

As the men finished their meal they were joined by the proprietor, who was as desirous to learn as much about his guests as they were anxious to orient themselves to the business of establishing a homestead in this foreign land.

"Our Dominion Lands Act is patterned after yours," announced Pat, "except that it's not quite as generous. Canada allows only one hundred and sixty acres after signing the affidavit, but you can apply for another adjacent one hundred and sixty acres after three years. Our Dominion Land Act divided the country into townships, each with thirty-six plots. None of the land where you want to homestead had been divided. In fact, there are not even any aerial photographs of that country. I don't know how the agent is going to handle your request. The Dominion Lands Act was actually designed to populate the prairie states, so I don't know how British Columbia fits in."

"How about supplies?" asked Barney. "Can we buy what we need here?"

"John, at the General Store will be happy to take your money," responded Pat. "He has everything, including every possible tool to get you started, but if you need machinery, he'll have to order it."

"We're here to hunt and trap, not raise crops," replied Louie, "But we'll need carpenter's tools to build a cabin. We will also need traps."

"I'd advise you to make a list tonight so you don't forget some important items. John has outfitted many a trapper, so he will be able to help you once he sees your list."

With that the conversation turned to trapping and living in the wilderness. Pat seemed to have knowledge about every trapper and prospector who had ever set out from Prince Rupert to make his fortune. To Pat, the types of adventures that Barney and Louie were about to attempt were foolish because they always resulted in failures of one type or another. Most of the adventuresome individuals about whom Pat spoke, if they returned at all, did so long before the trapping season was over, exhausted from trying to live off the land and discouraged with their harvest of furs. As they listened to Pat portraying the trappers who had gone before them, Barney and Louie concluded, each to himself, that he did not fit the categories of men described by Pat, nor did he possess the physical and mental characteristics that may have contributed to their failure. As the next three months would attest, self-assessment proved to be the most deceptive kind of evaluation.

The fifth day of the trappers' journey into Canada proved to be the most productive of their entire venture. The factor at the Dominion Land Office, too old to participate in the type of adventure envisioned by Barney and Louie, but still sufficiently young to live vicariously with them as they described their dream of achieving riches in the wilderness, took a liking to the two young men before him.

"So you want to turn your homestead into a trapping ground instead of a farm," he remarked, with a twinkle in his eye. "I'll have to see what we have available. I'm going to call Officer Mackenzie over to help us. He knows the country better than anyone here.

Let me go see if he's in." With that he walked down the hall to the office of the Royal Mounted Police. After nearly half and hour he returned with a tall, lean Mountie who looked as though he would be right at home living the life to which Barney and Louie had committed themselves.

"Men, this is Officer Mackenzie. He has patrolled this country for twenty years. He can tell you about the land, its animals, its rivers and lakes, and the problems that will do you in if you're not careful. Officer Mackenzie has agreed to take you to your homestead, but you will have to be ready to leave tomorrow morning. He will tell you the details of the trip, and what you need to take with you so you can survive the snow and cold. Officer Mackenzie, take these men to your office while I complete their paperwork." With that the factor dismissed the threesome and turned his attention to completing the affidavits the men had just requested.

"Men, follow me," commanded Officer Mackenzie, and he led them down the hall. Barney, six feet tall, found himself the shortest of the three, with Louie at six feet three inches, and Mountie Mackenzie at six feet four inches. "The factor asked me to find a suitable place for you to run your trapline. I know from reputation, an ideal place, but it is two hundred miles due east by train and then another four-day's ride by horseback north into the wilderness from there. The spot I have in mind is along the Skeena River, which should give you all the fur and meat you need. There won't be anyone else within forty miles of you. Are you sure you are interested in a place so far from any other human beings?"

Exchanging glances with Louie, Barney exclaimed, "It sounds like a great place to us. We'll get our supplies this afternoon and be ready to go tomorrow morning."

"Buy your supplies and then let me check the inventory," replied the Mountie. "I'll be at the General Store at three o'clock to check you out. Leave the supplies right at the store. I want to put them in packs before I take them down to the rail station, so I can see how many pack horses I will need to haul your stuff out to your homesteads."

Barney and Louie hurried to the General Store, anxious to buy their list of required items. The list they prepared contained the following items: one adz, one double-bit ax, one cross-cut saw, one whipsaw, one hand saw, two hammers, one mallet, one auger, one plane, two hand axes, one draw knife, two whetstones, two files, one twelve-gauge shotgun, one .30 Remington semiautomatic, two .22 caliber pistols, ammunition, fish hooks, line, two backpacks, thirty no. 1.5 traps, thirty no. 2 traps, ten pounds assorted nails, one Yukon stove, four lengths stovepipe, two windows, one washbasin, one broom, one bread pan, one bean pot, ten pounds of rice, fifty pounds of flour, ten pounds of sugar, ten pounds of salt, five pounds of tea, three small teapots, ten pounds of dried milk, ten pounds of dried eggs, ten pounds of pancake flour, six bars of soap, two agate plates, cups, forks, spoons, knives, one iron skillet, five pounds of laundry soap, twenty pounds of dried potatoes, yeast, five pounds of dried prunes, five pounds dried carrots, two glass windows, personal items such as caps, shirts, trousers, socks, rubber hip boots, pac boots, jackets, matches, smoking materials, rope, twine, thread, and needles.

Mountie Mackenzie appeared promptly at 3:00 p.m. and assured the trappers that their provisions were adequate for their time at the homestead. "I presume you will be eating fish, grouse, deer, moose, and elk for most of your meals," he commented.

"All you really need to survive is salt and flour as long as you can fish and hunt. I'll get your gear to the train that travels to the construction site when I head out two days from now. I have made arrangements for you to hunt game for the construction crew at Hazelton instead of having you pay for your ride out. Be ready to go at eight tomorrow morning. The foreman at the construction site is expecting you. He has rooms and meals for you during your three nights as hunters. On the fourth day, begin clearing a trail wide enough for the pack horses to get through, on the east side of the river. I'll catch up with you on your third night out." Having delivered his instructions, Mountie Mackenzie walked back to his office.

Sunrise the next morning found the homesteaders waiting at the train depot, ready for an adventure about which they could scarcely contain their excitement. The six-hour journey from Prince Rupert to Hazelton gave Barney and Louie a preview of the country in which they had chosen to spend the next three months. The train, carrying supplies to the construction crew at Hazelton, traveled eastward along the beautiful Skeena River, offering an unbroken view of forests for two hundred miles. This morning's destination was a site near Hazelton, where the river turned northward at its junction with the Babine River. The survey team and construction crew were reinforcing a trestle over a ravine so the tracks could continue on a level plane to Prince Albert.

Mountie Mackenzie had bartered a free ride to the construction site for Barney and Louie in exchange for a promise that the prospective trappers would supply meat to the protein-starved workers. Earlier in the summer the camp cooks had requisitioned a boxcar load of pigs, to be butchered on site as needed, only to have bears and wolves raid the pens on a regular basis. The lack of red meat on their menu had caused a minor rebellion among the construction workers.

In exchange for a ride to the jumping-off point for their homesteads, Barney and Louie had been hired to supply the camp cook with sufficient meat for the remainder of the fall construction project. Mountie Mackenzie had informed the trappers, "Ride out to the construction site. There are plenty of moose and deer in the area. Spend several days shooting enough animals to last the cooks for the season. I'll join you in six days with the horses and pack animals that we'll need to get to your homesteads. Take your axes and saws along. Four days from now start out along the east side of the river, clearing a path for the horses and pack animals. You'll see that the Skeena River turns due north just outside of Hazelton. Take some time to visit the totem poles near the Ksan Indian village. It's the best place in all of Canada to see the work of the native Canadians.

"By the end of the first night you will come to a rundown cabin. Clear away the trash and stay inside in case it rains. It's not pretty, but it beats getting wet. Take enough food for two days. The pack train and I will catch up with you before the evening of your second day on the trail. We'll camp under that rocky overhang the second night out, using food from the pack train. Then we'll have two more days of travel on horseback before we reach your homesteads."

When the train pulled into the construction site, Barney and Louie were greeted by a burly monster of a man, wearing a stained, white cook's apron. He strode forward and announced, "I'm Herm, the camp cook. You must be the meat hunters. If you can bring in some moose meat and venison, you will be heroes and possibly save my job. These men need red meat. They are cranky as hell and nothing I can cook satisfies them. Can you get started right away, so I have some meat to set out tonight?"

"Mountie Mackenzie said you would have rooms for us. Show us were we can change clothes, and we'll see what we can do," replied Barney.

As the men unloaded their gear, the cook spied Barney's rifle. "You can't shoot moose with that pea-shooter," he exclaimed, pointing to Barney's .30 caliber Remington.

"Why don't you wait until you see what I can shoot," retorted Barney, irritated at the cook's reference to his hunting ability. "Is all the country around here open to hunting?"

"Hunt anywhere you can find game," replied the cook. "Don't worry about dressing out the animals or bringing them out. My men have horses and pack saddles for that purpose. All you need to do is shoot some animals." Barney could tell from his condescending attitude that the cook doubted whether the hunters would be able to supply his request for meat.

Barney surveyed the area near the construction site for open spaces that animals, whether moose, deer or caribou, could use for grazing. Having located a meadow about a quarter mile from the site, he instructed Louie, armed with his shotgun, to circle the fir trees surrounding the field, with the intention of chasing any animals in the perimeter into the open field. Positioning himself in the woods seventy yards from a ravine that served as a natural pathway to the field, he waited for Louie to complete his circuit. He did not have long to wait. Hearing Louie shout, "Moose, moose, moose," Barney was ready when a herd of moose, running a full speed in response to Louie's urging, burst into the meadow from the ravine.

Six moose, five cows and a large bull, ran single file across the field. As they ran past Barney's concealed location in the pines, he systematically shot each animal through the head, resulting in a pile of dead moose within a ten-yard circle. Louie, having witnessed the spectacle from the ravine, ran up to Barney in admiration. "Where did you learn to shoot like that?" he asked.

"I've been shooting since I was twelve years old. We didn't have money to waste on ammunition, so I had to shoot straight or go home empty-handed," replied Barney. "Now let's go show the cook what this pea-shooter just did."

The six moose lying in the small area filled the cook with awe and admiration. "Barney, I'll eat my words about you as a hunter. I can tell you have experience as a shooter. I've learned my lesson about ridiculing another man's rifle." The cook's crew was also happy to see the animals lying in the open meadow, instead of having to search the woods for the downed game. That evening Barney and Louie were the toast of the construction crew as they feasted on moose steaks. Stories about Barney's remarkable ability of shooting each of the running moose through the head circulated throughout the mess hall that evening.

After several more days of hunting, Herm announced, "That's enough game for the season," as Barney and Louie continued to provide deer and moose for the cook's larder.

"Good," replied Barney. "We have to leave tomorrow for our homesteads. Mountie Mackenzie will be here two days later with horses and pack animals. We'll see you in December, and maybe hit you up for a steak, if you have any left."

"It's a deal if we're still here. Time for us leaving here will depend on the weather. Thanks for helping me feed the men. They sure are enjoying the meat. Good luck in the homesteading." With that the big cook, now considerably more friendly than on their first meeting, disappeared into the cook's shanty.

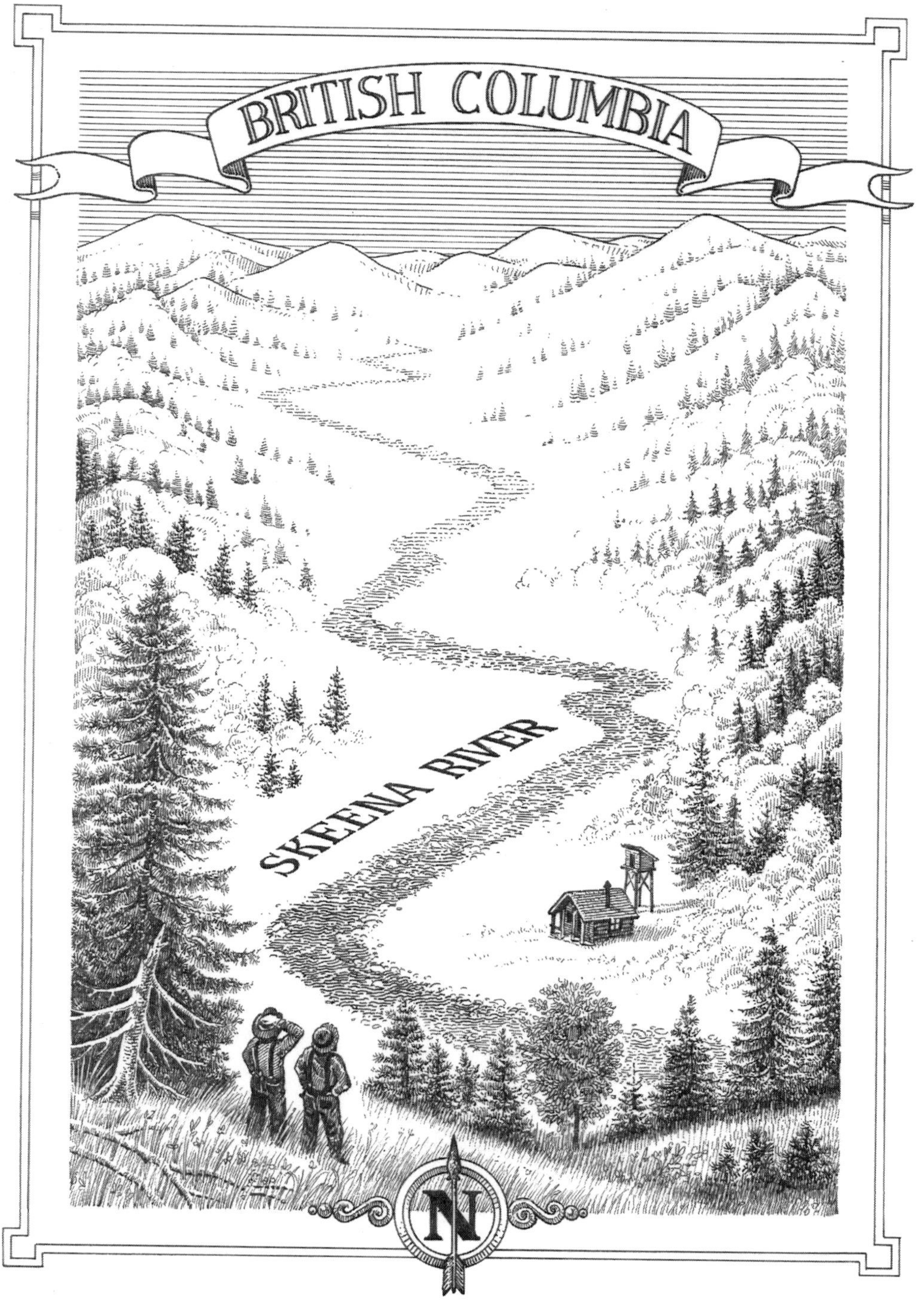
BRITISH COLUMBIA
SKEENA RIVER
N

Chapter 4

Selecting the Homestead

"There it is," announced Mountie Mackenzie, seemingly to himself, as he reined in his horse on the crest of a gentle hill overlooking a large valley. Mackenzie's four-day journey had brought the trio to the edge of the Skeena valley that seemed to extend for miles. The four pack animals tethered behind Mackenzie's horse stopped, weary in their tracks, anticipating an end to the trek which had taken them across countless boulders and windfalls that littered the path along the Sheena River. Anxious to see their new homestead, Barney and Louie quickly dismounted their horses and ran to the front of the pack train where Scott Mackenzie was surveying the vast country that lay before him.

Overcome with the awesome spectacle that met their gaze, Barney and Louie stared speechless with delight upon the most beautiful country that either had ever seen. The glowing Skeena River winded its way through the valley until it disappeared into a forest of cedar and spruce trees to the far north. The valley consisted of a large, flat plain that at one time had been completely under water, but now was teeming with trees and vegetation that flourished on the sediment that had been left by the receding glacier thousands of years ago.

The area next to the river was overgrown with willow and pucker brush, now in their autumn shades of brown, yellow, and red. A short distance beyond the river the elevating surface of the valley was interspersed with stands of aspens, which too, were in their golden fall colors. Beyond the aspens on the higher ground on all sides of the valley lay the dark green forests of cedar, spruce, and hemlock. Surrounding the valley on three sides jutted the snow-capped peaks of the Skeena Mountains. The spectacle before them was so overwhelming that Barney and Louie, accustomed to beauty of the outdoors, stared spellbound at the awe-inspiring landscape before them.

"All of this is ours?" asked Barney in disbelief over the prospect of owning land in the beautiful valley.

"No, only the country on the east side of the river is yours, and not all that you can see from here is yours. It's twenty miles to the foot of those mountains in the west, and an additional seventy miles to the farthest peaks in the north," replied Mackenzie. "In the next couple of days, we'll survey the area and then I can tell you exactly where your homesteads are located. In the meantime, let's get down to the river and get these horses unpacked. The hour of daylight left will give us time to set up camp and take care of the horses." Never one to waste time, Mackenzie gave a tug on the reins and sent his horse and the pack train down the hill toward the small, grassy meadow that lay above the gray boulders that lined the riverbed.

Barney, an avid brook trout fisherman, hurried to the head of the convoy in an attempt to see the water before it was disturbed by the horses. He need not have hurried because as the hoof beats of the horses shook the overhanging banks of the river, the water churned as dozens of trout fled to the safety of deeper water. As Barney followed the flight of the trout toward a large pool, he could hardly believe what he saw. There, in a pool about seven-feet deep, suspended about a foot from the bottom of the clear water lay several dozen trout, each about twenty to twenty-four inches long.

"Look at those trout," exclaimed Barney to Mackenzie, who had followed the pack animals to the river.

"Big trout like that die of old age around here," remarked Mackenzie. "They have only one natural enemy-otters-if they stay in the deep water. The mink and raccoons feed on the fingerlings in the shallow water, but nothing bothers the big ones. We don't even have predator fish like pike, muskies, or bass up here to weed out the weak ones."

"I brought a telescope rod and a small reel," offered Barney. "I'll try to catch some of the big ones for supper."

"You won't be able to bring in any of those six-pounders unless you have the right equipment," explained Mackenzie. "If we have time tomorrow I'll show you how we catch big fish up here. Now let's get our camp set up."

The site that Mountie Mackenzie selected for the evening's campsite was a smooth, grass-laden slope about a hundred feet from the river. Years of experience in the Canadian north woods had taught him that a good campsite required four essentials—a spring or fast flowing source of water, a dry place above the run-off in case of rain, dry firewood nearby, and grass for the horses. His vast knowledge of the geography associated with mountains and rivers told him their present location had all of the requisites, and therefore, negated any need to travel farther that evening. With the discretion accorded him by the land office, he had determined that this location would be well suited to fit the dreams of Barney and Louie.

Within minutes the tired horses, relieved of their burdens, and refreshed by the river water, were hobbled and turned loose so they could feed on the abundant grass. Eager and efficient hands soon had the eight packs stacked inside a canvas lean-to, which would also serve as a mobile shelter until the homesteaders' cabins were finished. A fire of pine knots soon heated the evening's simple meal of canned meat and the trapper's staple of pork and beans. Hot water for tea and pipes of tobacco completed the evening meal. As was the custom of men in the wilderness, words were at a premium until all of the chores were completed. Each man knew from experience what needed to be done and went about doing his part in silence.

"Better get some sleep," advised Mackenzie after the dishes had been scrubbed with the fine sand that formed the banks of the river and rinsed in the ice-cold water. "It's already nine o'clock, and we have several days of hard work ahead of us. Surveying the country to mark off your homesteads won't be a picnic. And after I'm gone you two will have several weeks of really tough work, building your cabins."

"The work would go much faster if you stayed and helped us," joked Barney, knowing that Mackenzie had to return to his post in Prince Rupert.

"I'd like nothing better than to spend some time out here in this beautiful valley," replied Mackenzie. "But the legislators in Ottawa didn't put that in my job description. I have to be back at the post a week from now, and if the horses don't get scared off by a grizzly bear on my way out, I'll make it with time to spare."

"Tell me," chimed in Louie, tired, but too excited to sleep, "How did you know that this spot was the place for our homesteads? You didn't take any measurements. We just rode for four days beyond the place where the railroad construction crews were working."

"Tell you the truth, I don't know exactly," replied McKenzie. "I talked to the head of the railroad survey crew before I caught up with you. He told me that fifty-seven degrees latitude would be about four-day's ride by horseback from Hazelton and a day's ride north of where the Babine River joins the Skeena. He told me that the longitude for your homesteads would be about four days' ride from the railroad construction site, and this is four days' ride. Are you complaining about the site I chose for you?" replied Mackenzie, winking at Barney.

"Gosh, no," exclaimed Louie. "You picked the prettiest, most ideal place in all the country. But I was curious how you could choose this spot, knowing you hadn't been here before and didn't use any surveying tools as we rode along."

"This business of assigning homesteads according to precise geographical locations will be a bit hazardous until we have aerial photographs of the entire country and that will take a few more years," replied McKenzie. "I knew about this spot because an old prospector told me about it many years ago. He raved about it so much that I always wanted to see it. When the land office talked to me about your intentions, I suggested to them that this would be a good spot for you. Truth of the matter is, the old fellow said there are several more just as pretty beyond this point, but I figured this will keep you away from any travelers for some time to come."

"But no matter how the aerial survey turns out, if they ever get to it, no one will be able to move you off your homesteads. There is a law in Canada to prevent takeovers of previous settlements by late comers. We treat our settlers a little better than you did the Indians in your country," chided Mackenzie, who was well aware of the history that surrounded the Indian wars in the United States and also of the brief skirmishes involving Canadian settlers with Indians during the Riel Rebellion in the 1870–1880s.

The next two days found Scott Mackenzie, Barney, and Louie busy with compass, survey wheel, metal stakes, and maul in hand. Arising at sunrise each morning, which occurred at five thirty, they consumed a hearty breakfast of powdered eggs, bacon, bannock, and black coffee. After leading the horses to drink at the river and back to the grassy hillside, the men returned to the east bank of the Skenna River to begin the day's work.

The anchor point from which Scott Mackenzie began his measurements was an arbitrary location that included the hillside from which the three adventurers had first seen the beautiful valley. It also included a flood plain of gravel that led upward to a stand of cedar and hemlock trees. More by design than accident, Scott Mackenzie had entered the valley at a place that was an ideal site for one of the cabins. With plenty of mature trees for the cabin, and gravel to serve as its base, Barney and Louie begin to suspect that Scott Mackenzie was more than a usual representative of the Canadian Government. Each now realized that their guide had taken a liking to them and was doing all he could to ensure that their adventure would be successful.

"My record tells me that the homestead farthest to the south is yours, Barney," announced Mackenzie. "You were the first to file, and the land office assigned the southern-most Homesteader's deed to you."

"You'll get no argument from either of us about where you tell us to place the stakes, given the kind of country we're about to claim," announced Barney.

"I'm glad the first one is Barney's. That will bring my land closer to the beaver dams," joshed Louie, so enthralled with the thought of owning a piece of the magnificent country that any assignment would have pleased him.

"OK, then. Let's start here," announced Mackenzie, pointing to a place free of boulders several yards above the river's edge. "Barney, you get to drive the stakes for your own homestead."

Moving along the Skeena River, the three men took turns, rolling the survey wheel northward while the other two cleared away fallen trees, boulders, and occasionally, the debris around a beaver's lodge. Finally, Scott Mackenzie announced, "OK, the wheel tells me we've come far enough. Barney, this is the northern edge of your homestead. Drive a stake here."

"Louie, drive another stake next to Barney's" continued Mackenzie. "This marks the southern edge of your homestead. Let's travel along the river, and I'll tell you when we've officially marked the south-to-north boundaries of your land. Then we'll see how far east into the valley your property runs."

By mid-afternoon the stakes that marked the northern borders of both homesteads were in place. The hot sun had caused the two homesteaders to shed their shirts. Red skin on their shoulders caused Mackenzie to issue a warning, "Men, even though we're a long ways north of the equator, the sun can still burn your skin so badly you won't sleep tonight. Let's go take a swim, and when we get back, it'll be cool enough to put your shirts back on." Refreshed by the cold waters of the Skeena River, the homesteaders realized that Mackenzie had wisely provided a tonic that permitted them to work far into the evening before retiring.

Establishing the eastern borders of the homesteads proved to be much more difficult than the previous task of mercy reversing the north-to-south flow of the river and measuring the distance in rods. Scott Mackenzie insisted that the route along the eastern borders of the homesteads be accessible via horseback, which entailed clearing a path eight feet wide along the heart of the valley. In addition, he announced that part of the Homesteader's ordinance directed that all borders must be clearly identifiable. To Mackenzie, such a mandate meant that all borders of the homesteads must also be cleared of trees, brush, and fallen logs. Fortunately, the skills of the two former lumberjacks, combined with their muscular prowess and eagerness to complete the task made short work of felling trees, cutting them into sections and clearing a pathway. Mackenzie, with his surveyor's wheel and compass, had to hurry to stay ahead of the two newly created homesteaders as they blazed the trail that marked the boundaries of their land.

By the end of the second day the task of marking and clearing the boundaries was completed. After the evening meal Scott Mackenzie announced, "Men, early tomorrow morning I'll be on my way back to civilization. You two are now well situated. You have shown me that you can take care of yourselves. I've never set up anyone in a homestead, especially this far north, in whom I've had greater confidence. You'll do fine and should make lots of money, if the signs we saw in the last two days are an indication of the fur in this country."

"We sure do thank you for all you've done," replied Barney. "We'll make it up to you when we get back to Prince Rupert."

"We'll be sure to look you up when the snow gets too deep out here," added Louie.

This remark drew a caution from Mackenzie. "Remember, once the deep snow sets in, which will be in early December, you won't be able to get out, and nobody will be able to reach you. You have only brought enough supplies to last you through November. After that you will have to live without salt, sugar, flour, and canned goods. You can always live off trout, moose, and deer, so you won't starve, but the living won't be good."

"Scott, we have no intention of staying past the first of December," announced Louie. "Besides, I want to see what kind of girls you keep in Prince Rupert during the winter. Five months of loafing and loving sounds like my kind of living."

"It gets pretty dark and lonely in Prince Rupert, too, but it sure beats sitting in a cabin out here, with snow up to the roof and nary a thing to do but chop ice for your water and listen to the wind blow," replied Mackenzie. With that, Mountie Mackenzie emptied his pipe and walked under the tarp that had been his home for several days. Wrapping a blanket over his long frame, he turned his back on the two prospective trappers and nestled into the grassy mattress as if it were a down comforter. Within seconds his heavy breathing told Barney and Louie that he had fallen asleep.

The two excited landowners knew that they, too, should follow Mackenzie's example of sleeping whenever the opportunity presented itself, but the prospects of building cabins and laying out their trapline proved to be too stimulating for either of them to defer such thoughts until the next day. Several pipes of tobacco were consumed, with only the light of the glowing embers to illuminate their animated faces as they discussed in hushed tones the prospects of the next few months. Where would they build the cabins? What kind of cabins would they build? Where would they set their traps? Would their skills as trappers be a match for the game in the area? How would each man handle the loneliness of the trapline? Barney was convinced that he could deal with the lack of human contact for three months, but he began to wonder if Louie's constant need for social stimulation would become a problem.

When the creatures of the night-the wolves, the coyotes, and owls-announced by their calls that it was time to hunt, Barney and Louie extinguished their pipes and reluctantly joined Scott Mackenzie under the canvas tarp that also served as a shelter for their supplies. However, Barney's recent conversation with Louie had aroused an uneasy feeling about Louie's readiness for three solitary months in the wilderness. Louie's questions about living alone in the outdoors, and his knowledge about trapping were especially worrisome to Barney. Perhaps the days ahead would reveal just how much fantasy Louie had provided in their previous discussions about trapping.

Early the next morning Barney and Louie were awakened by the smell of frying bacon and the aroma of boiling coffee. "Come on, you sleepyheads," called Mackenzie, "time's a-wasting."

"Do you always get up before sunrise?" asked Louie, whose sleep had been interrupted by dreams of encounters with grizzly bears and wolves.

"Usually not, but when I'm faced with twelve hours in the saddle, it's good to get an early start," responded Mackenzie.

"How far will you ride today?" asked Barney.

"I'm hoping to get to the survey stake by seven tonight. It took us two days to get from there to here, but with a clean trail and empty pack saddles I'll be able to move twice as fast. I'll camp under the canopy of that rocky overhang. That will give me cover, in case it rains. Then tomorrow I'll get to that abandoned cabin, where I'll spend the night. By Wednesday I hope to sleep in a cabin at the construction site. The next day I'll load the horses on a box car and reach Prince Rupert about six hours after the engineer decides it time to head for home."

"Sure you won't need any help with the horses?" asked Barney.

"Heck, no!" responded Mackenzie. "They know they're going home. I'll keep ole Sally's halter rope tied to my saddle, and the rest won't stray far from her. Same is true in the evenings. As long as we're in grizzly country, the horses won't wonder too far from my campfire."

Breakfast that morning lacked the congenial atmosphere commonly associated with previous meals the three-some had shared around an open fire. Barney and Louie had grown genuinely fond of their new friend. Both knew that Mountie Mackenzie had provided them with homestead sites for which they could never repay him. They were also impressed by Mackenzie's knowledge of the wilderness, and his efficient way of living within the laws of nature. Each had plied the Mountie with countless questions during the time they had spent beside their evening and morning campfires. Both realized there would be numerous situations in the weeks ahead where Mackenzie's expertise would be invaluable, but from now on they would have to depend on their own resources.

"Well, time to go," announced Mackenzie. "Give me a hand in rounding up the horses and then I'll be off." The horses responded eagerly to the call for their daily share of ground oats, almost as if they knew that the trip home would be easier than the grueling journey of a week ago. The empty saddles and pack frames were a welcome relief from the heavy burdens they had carried over the treacherous trails leading to the homesteads.

Minutes later Mackenzie mounted his big sorrel, pulled gently on Sally's rope and the line of horses behind him moved down the slope toward the river. Just before Mackenzie entered the grove of cedars that would hide him from view he rose in the stirrups, looked back at the two homesteaders and waved. In another minute the forest swallowed up the last of the pack animals and erased any further opportunities for Barney and Louie to communicate with the outside world. Neither anticipated that the next four months would test their mental and physical capacities in ways they could not imagine at the present time.

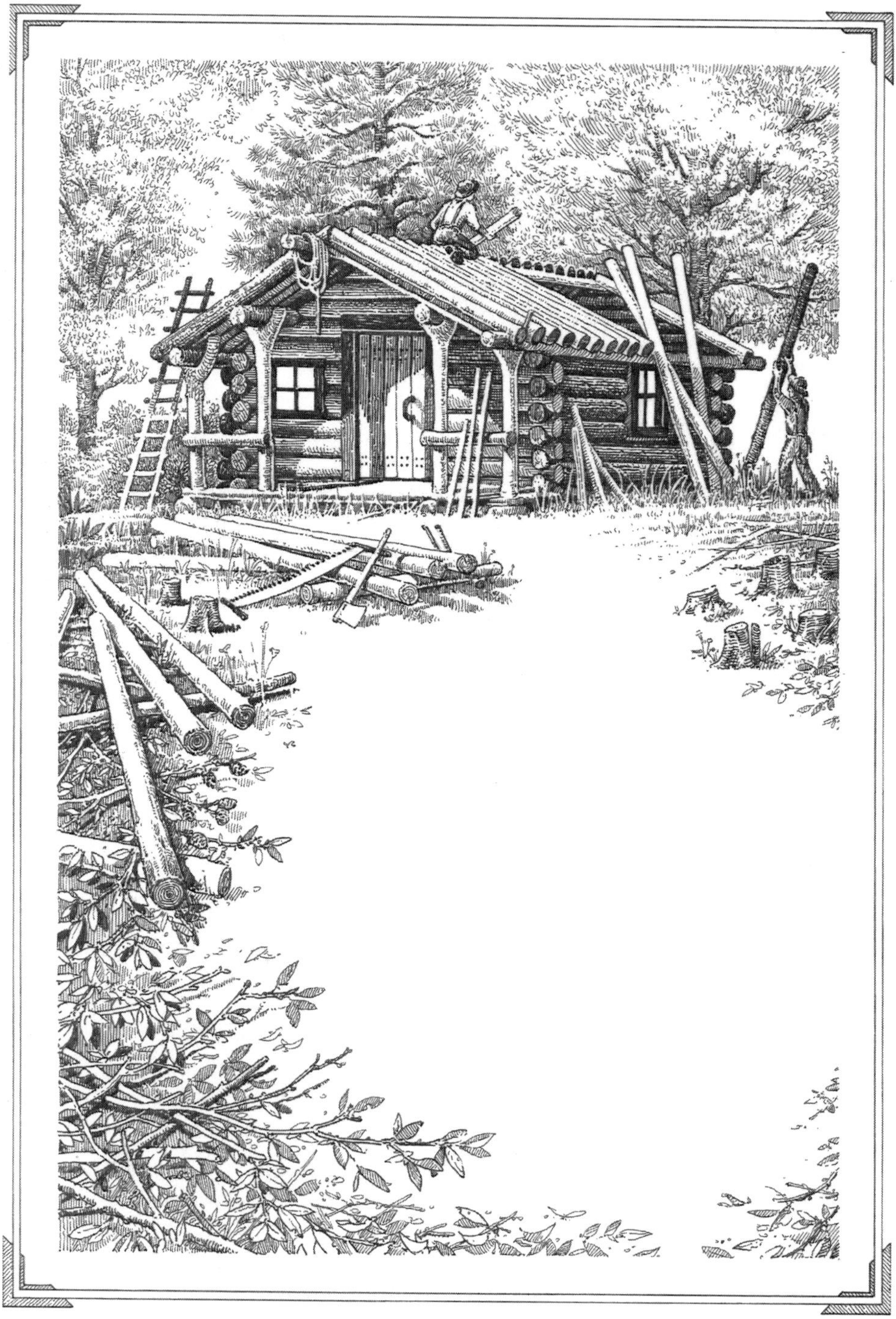

Chapter 5

Building the Cabin

As Scott Mackenzie's pack animals disappeared into the growth of young cedars Barney and Louie were momentarily overwhelmed with the realization that they were now alone in the wilderness. They were actually eighty miles from the railroad construction site and nearly three hundred miles from Prince Rupert. This acknowledgment brought home the sobering reminder that self-reliance was now their key to survival. They also fully understood the consequences of spending an additional week in the Fargo wheat fields at the behest of farmer Lorenz. Their late arrival in Prince Rupert, combined with the delay in obtaining permission and filing for homesteads had prolonged the trip to their homesteads by three weeks-a mistake that each would come to regret in the coming months as the weather changed from the balmy days of September to the bone-chilling cold of November.

High in the northwestern sky a large V-shaped flock of Canada geese was moving south to its destination in southern California. Their honking brought Barney and Louie out of their momentary lapse in concentration and back to the reality that could no longer be avoided.

"We had better get a move on," remarked Barney, ever ready to account for the productivity of each day's activities. "The trapping season opens next week, and we don't have cabins nor do we know where we're going to set our traps."

"Let's take a few days to enjoy this. We can always build for part of the day and then finish the cabins as we trap," suggested Louie, with a nonchalance that irritated Barney.

"I think we'll find that running a trapline will be more than a full-time job for both of us," retorted Barney. "By my reasoning, we're at least three weeks behind schedule." This latest remark by Louie reinforced Barney's concern that Louie did not really understand the rigors imposed by a trapline.

"Well, then, let's start today with the first cabin and see how long it takes two experienced carpenters like us to put one up," countered the ever-optimistic Louie, who by now had learned that it was futile to resist Barney's insistence on careful day-to-day and long-range planning.

"On whose homestead shall we start?" asked Barney as though he had already determined the answer. "Because all the tools, supplies, and the tent are here, it makes sense to build the first cabin right where we're standing."

"I agree," responded the easy-going Louie, knowing full well that such a decision meant that the first cabin would be built on Barney's land. Any decision that would keep the two homesteaders from any confrontations in their adventure suited him just fine. Besides, he was ready to go where destiny, in this case, Barney's directives, led him.

Once the decision was made to build a cabin on the site where they had entered the beautiful Sheena Valley, the two men located the tools that had been so carefully selected in Prince Rupert and packed with such care for the trip. The reverence with which the two former carpenters unpacked and inspected the invaluable tools told of their appreciation for the quality of good instruments. As carpenters, they knew the value of keeping their tools razor sharp. Both men insisted that each day's work begin with tools that were in perfect condition.

"Well, everything seems to have survived the trip in good shape," assessed Barney. "We won't even have to sharpen the axes and saws. The way the packs bounced and scraped off the trees during the ride in here made me think that we would have to spend the morning with files and grinding stones instead of getting started on the trees."

"Ole Sally did a better job of protecting our instruments than we gave her credit for," replied Louie. "I thought for sure when she skidded down that slope our tools were goners. Any horse in the Midwest would have tossed the load and saved its skin, but Sally showed us what she was made of."

"I don't blame Scott from wanting to take her home with him," said Barney, in reference to the homesteader's suggestion that leaving one of the horses behind would be extremely useful when it came time to hauling the timbers down to the cabin site. Mackenzie had dismissed the suggestion, stating that the horse would surely find its way back to civilization before winter, but the numerous cougars and grizzly bears en route would make such a trip for a lone horse extremely hazardous. "Sally has been so good to me for so long that I just can't abandon her now," had been Mackenzie's reaction. Barney and Louie's appreciation for the value of good horses ended the discussion. The thought of leaving any horses behind was not broached again.

With cross-cut saw, adz, broad ax, double-bladed axes, and draw knife in hand, the two men strode toward the stand of cedar and hemlock trees which stood a mere one hundred feet from the proposed cabin site. Careful scrutiny of the trees on the hillside indicated that there were a sufficient number of hemlock trees for the base of the cabin and abundant cedars for the upper walls, floor, and roof. The homesteaders decided that the cabin dimensions of 14' × 20' would provide enough room for their immediate needs and yet be manageable from the standpoint of raising the lighter cedar logs to the upper levels of the building.

With the efficiency of skilled lumberjacks, Barney and Louie felled all the trees needed for the cabin in one day. The chips flew as the loggers, one on each side of the large trees, cut the notches that indicated the precise direction where the trees would fall. As the cross-cut saw ripped through the backside of the trees it became apparent that the two displaced lumberjacks knew exactly where each tree would fall before the first blows of the axes determined its fate.

Barney's skill as a visionary carpenter became apparent once the trees were felled. By arranging the logs in parallel fashion on the ground, he was able to simulate the four sides of the cabin. Thus, the entire cabin was visually and literally assembled before the logs were moved to the cabin site. With adz and broad ax the two carpenters were able to hew the lower and upper surfaces of the logs and notch the ends on the site where the trees were felled. This ability to accurately arrange the final form of the cabin while it was in its unassembled state was a skill that Barney had learned from his mentor, Goetlieb Gannigan, whose ability to arrange the preassembled pieces of barns and sheds into perfect structures before they were erected was legendary. Final preparation of the logs off-site also kept the bark and chips away from the actual cabin site and reduced the energy required to move the logs down the slope to their final destination.

By the end of the second day, the logs for the floor and sides of the cabin had been hewed, and their ends notched into smooth-fitting cross-pieces. Next the carpenters built a platform for the purpose of holding elevated logs in place—a position from which they were sawed lengthwise into boards for the roof. The large cedar logs were then hoisted onto the elevated platform, until one by one they contributed to the large pile of planks that would soon be fastened by pegs to the cedar rafters to form the roof. This primitive process of making planks and boards from logs, known as whipsawing, was the most undesirable task involved in building the cabin. One of the carpenters stood beneath, and one on the platform and commenced sawing planks from the lengthwise sections of the logs.

The large cedar trunks yielded planks that were two inches thick, fourteen to sixteen inches in width, and twenty feet long. Despite the falling sawdust involved in whipsawing, this procedure provided planks for a smooth, strong surface to bear the weight of snow on the roof, which Mountie Mackenzie told them would accumulate to a depth of four feet. Using a broad ax, the carpenters next split blocks of cedar trunks into shingles a foot square and two inches thick, which would cover the planks to ensure that the melting snow and ice did not penetrate the cabin's interior.

Cutting four logs to be used as rollers and laying the cabin's logs perpendicular to the rollers, the two homesteaders soon transferred the logs down the slope to the flood plane of the river. Next they dug a trench two feet deep into the pea gravel that covered the surface of the flood plane. Into the trench they placed hemlock logs that had been hewn flat on two sides. These logs, which served as the foundation of the cabin, were fastened on each end to perpendicular logs by pounding pegs of oak wood into holes that had been drilled into the notched ends of each log. Inside this foundation of logs, on top of the pea gravel, the two men placed cedar logs side by side, hewn smooth on four sides, which became the floor of the cabin.

The erection phase of constructing the cabin was accomplished with ease because of Louie's enormous strength. Whenever a log needed to be moved, Louie merely grasped the trunk with his gigantic hands, wrapped his arms around it, and with a forceful extension of his powerful legs, moved the log into place. Barney, himself a man of greater than usual strength, marveled at the ease with which his companion lifted the huge timbers into their notched receptacles.

"I can see where I was wrong in asking Mackenzie to loan us a horse," remarked Barney in awe, "We won't need one if your back lasts another few days."

"I've always loved lifting," remarked Louie. "I was a member of a high school wrestling team for a little while when I was fifteen, but the coach told me that most of the moves I used to throw down my teammates were illegal, so I quit."

"Remind me to never get in a situation where you want to wrestle with me," said Barney, who had seen his share of Saturday night barroom brawls as a lumberjack, but he had never seen anyone who could compare with Louie in strength and agility. "I don't know of any two men who could lift the loads that you've been lifting out here."

"Fair enough," replied the congenial Louie. "You handle the adz and the broad ax and tell me where you want the logs, and we'll get this cabin up in no time."

By the end of the seventh day, the two men had erected the logs on the four sides of the cabin to a height of seven feet, completed the gable ends, placed the rough-sawn planks in place as roof boards, and shingled the cabin. To add a finishing touch, they fitted a hollowed-out log along the peak of the roof as a ridge pole and installed an asbestos liner around the hole where the stove pipe emerged from the cabin. An eight-foot overhang facing the river protected the entrance from rain and snow. Two recessed windows with glass panes lent a civilized look to the front and rear of the cabin, allowing a little of the precious light to enter the bare, cedar-scented cabin.

"I wish we could have persuaded Scott to let us bring four windows," said Barney after inspecting the dark interior of the cabin.

"He didn't think we'd even get the two we have out here without breaking them," replied Louie. "He said oil cloth and shutters worked better than glass, anyway. Besides, we won't be in the cabin during the day, and in the evening, we'll have candles. By December, when the wind howls out of the north, we may wish we had taken his advice and used shutters."

"Well, let's get those iron bars on the windows and call it a day," replied Barney. "Tomorrow we can build bunks and move in. Right now, I'm going to celebrate by taking a plunge in the river. Coming?"

"Yep," replied Louie, grabbing a towel from his knapsack. "I'm going to wash these clothes at the same time. Pretty soon the water will be too cold for our evening swims. I look forward to the dip in the river as the best part of the day."

"I know, but when that time comes, we'll use the stove to heat water," said Barney.

"Besides, our days of sweating through our shirts are nearly over. Pretty soon we'll have to work hard just to keep warm, much less worry about sweating."

"Remember what Scott told us about sweating," replied Louie. "He said the Eskimos and Indians up here keep from freezing because they deliberately never run or even walk fast enough to sweat. We should remember that when we get out on the trap lines."

"Good advice," replied Barney. "I'll remind you of that when you come upon your first grizzly. But knowing you, you'll probably try to wrestle it."

"Not me," retorted Louie. "The grizzlies were here first, and as far as I'm concerned, it's still their country. Now how about that swim?"

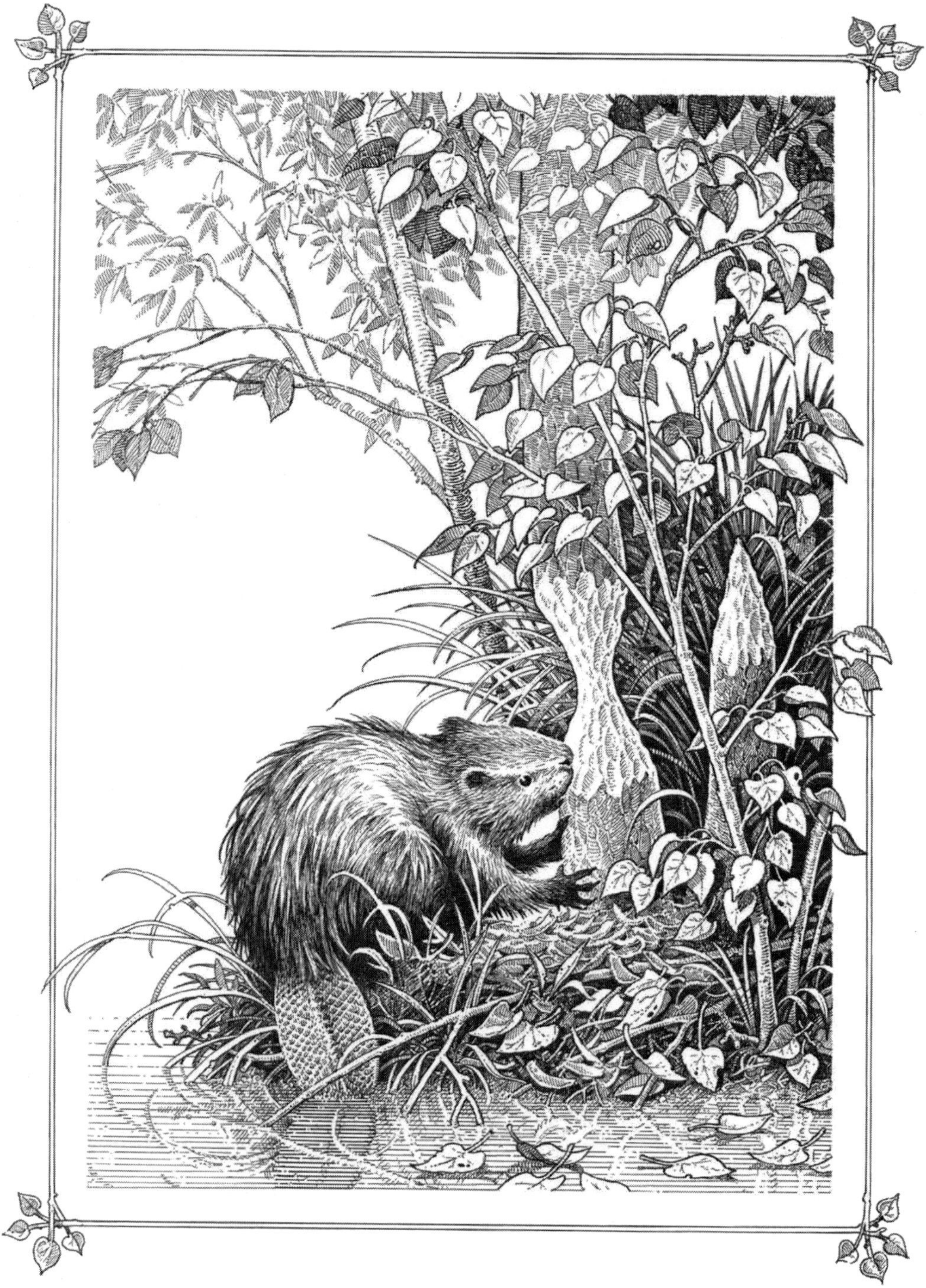

Chapter 6

Success on the Trapline

"Hey, Louie, do you know what day it is?" asked Barney as he tossed aside his Hudson Bay blanket and reached for his boots.

"No, but I suppose it's one of your girlfriends' birthday," remarked Louie, who was so overwhelmed by the freedom of the wilderness that he purposely let time roll by without paying attention to the days or weeks.

"It's the opening day of the trapping season," remarked Barney. "And we don't even have our traps unpacked."

"This may surprise you," said Louie, "But I have been thinking about our timetable and all of the work yet to be done. I think we should forget about the second cabin and share this one. Next spring when the snow is gone we can come out and take our time building the one on my homestead and improving this one."

"That makes good sense to me," replied Barney. "If we spend another week to ten days building the second cabin, we will really be late in getting our traps out. Let's start scouting the territory for our trapline today and see if we can get our traps set in the next few days."

After a hurried breakfast the two trappers packed food, blankets, and traps into their knapsacks and set off for an estimated two-day exploration of their prospective trapline. Barney, carrying his .30 Remington, led the way, while Louie followed a few paces behind, armed with his twelve gauge pump shotgun, with which they intended to bag ptarmigan for their evening meal. Exploration of the marshes, streams, and woodlands that constituted their combined homesteads convinced the two men that the territory teemed with large and small game.

The constant activity of deer and moose had worn deep, wide paths leading to the river. Beaver lodges could be seen along the riverbanks every several hundred yards. Each of the four streams leading into the Skenna River from the east in what was now the trappers' homestead was blocked by a beaver dam, forming large pools behind the dams. Tracks of mink, muskrats, otters, and raccoons in the muddy trails that led to the water indicated that these animals were hunting for food in the areas where water had flooded the low land surrounding the dams.

"I've already found enough places to set my thirty traps," joked Barney, after two hours of their excursion. His experienced eye told him that the valley offered abundant places to catch the small furbearers from which they intended to reap a fortune.

"And we haven't even been to the high country yet," reminded Louie. "Besides trapping beaver, I think some of the easiest money to be made is by trapping the fisher and pine marten that we'll find up there."

"I'm not so sure," replied Barney. "My experience in Wisconsin taught me that beaver and mink were a lot easier to deal with than fisher and pine martins. Not because they are harder to catch, but when you get to the high country you have to figure on the fishers, along with the wolverine, foxes, wolves, and bears raiding the traps, stealing our bait and sometimes even eating the animals we've caught."

"Well, I'm going to try to catch a silver fox, which Scott Mackenzie said will bring three hundred dollars," remarked the congenial Louie.

"By the way, Louie, we will have to decide how much trapline we can cover," cautioned Barney. "We can't extend it forever. Remember, we have only one cabin and one cache in which to store our furs. Catching all these animals won't do any good without some way to store and protect their fur until we get to Prince Rupert."

"I've been thinking about that, too," said Louie. "How about setting thirty traps in the water and the other thirty on the high ground. Then we won't have to worry about over-trapping our homesteads, which is another danger about which Mackenzie warned us."

"Are you suggesting that we set traps beyond the boundaries of our homesteads?" asked Barney.

"Certainly," responded Louie. "Remember, Mackenzie said there was no law against trapping anywhere in this country because it is all considered to be Crown land unless someone has a legal claim to it. And he said that no one has filed a claim in this area."

"I'll agree with your suggestion of setting our traps in only the best places," replied Barney. "But I don't think, we should go very far beyond our land with our traps."

"Let's see what the country to the north and east of our homesteads looks like," suggested Louie, knowing that only the abundant signs of animals, and not words, were likely to persuade Barney to move the trapline far beyond their property.

With that, the two trappers shouldered their packs and set off to explore the high ground that marked the extreme eastern boundary of their homesteads. To their delight, signs of large and small game were everywhere. Deer and moose stood and gazed at them and trotted off only when the trappers approached to within a hundred feet. Frequent claw marks seven-feet high on the cedar trees, evidence of large bears in the area, dampened the trappers' enthusiasm momentarily, but the abundant signs of foxes, marten, and wolverines soon restored their optimistic expectations of success. As the evening sun signaled the end of the day's exploration, the two tired trappers settled under the protective cover of a rocky overhang and built their evening fire.

The day of discovery had exceeded their expectations, but Barney was concerned that it may also have led to the possibility of expanding their trapline beyond their abilities to adequately cover the territory. He had a premonition that Louie's propensity for exploring the unknown had been aroused by the day's activities. Louie seemed desirous of traveling ever northward in the beautiful valley, oblivious of the time it would take to cover the distance involved and at the same time attend to their traps. He made a mental note that when they had completed the circuit he would again urge Louie to be cautious about extending the trapline into unknown areas.

"If we include all of the country we've covered in the last two days as part of our trapline it will take us at least three days to make one complete circuit," estimated Barney.

"So be it," remarked Louie. "I'll gladly stay out two nights if that gets us more furs. Besides, we can build shelters that are nearly as good as cabins, with all the trees and windfalls in the area. And it will only take us an hour or so to build each one."

"That means all of our traps won't be covered everyday," cautioned Barney. "A three day trapline means that on one of the three days neither of us will visit certain traps. And once we start trapping on that schedule, we won't see each other until the end of the season."

"I'll write long letters to you on birch bark," joked Louie. "Really, Barney, we both wanted to see if we can survive out here and get rich while we're doing it. What better test can we have? If something happens we can always use gunshots or smoke as a signal. We're only one or two days, cross country, away from each other, and both of us ought to be able to make it alone under those conditions."

Barney knew that the ideal conditions about which Louie was fantasizing would not materialize once the snow and cold set in, but at the moment he was content to let Louie learn from firsthand experience—a decision that he would come to regret in the months and years ahead.

"Getting to know you during the last four weeks tells me that I am much more suited to talking with the animals than you are," observed Barney, who knew of Louie's love for conversation with anybody and everybody that crossed his path. "You've never met anyone that you didn't like or with whom you didn't strike up a conversation."

"It will give me time to practice my whistling, and I'll use my harmonica to practice some of the new tunes you taught me," suggested Louie, not entirely in jest. Both Louie and Barney were outstanding harmonica players and had frequently entertained themselves around the evening campfire with their pocket-sized instruments.

"If that is what we want to do, we will have to decide on a system of letting each other know what is going on with the traps-leaving messages-so that we don't waste days having both of us in the same place just because we need to talk," suggested Barney. "How about building small caches for written messages at the two outposts and using a system of blazes to indicate when and where we move our traps?"

"Good idea," remarked Louie. "We have pencils. And the birch bark that seems to be everywhere will serve as paper."

"OK," replied Barney. "Now let's get some sleep. Tomorrow we need to decide how we're going to set the different kinds of traps.

Catching mink, beaver, marten, fisher, and foxes each requires different sets."

"If you say so," replied Louie, whose reluctance to further the conversation suggested to Barney that Louie did not have as much trapping experience as he had previously implied. "I'm ready for some lessons, but right now, I'm going to see how this mattress of balsam boughs works on this piece of rock that you chose for our campsite."

"Good night, Louie. If you can sleep with those coyotes yipping, you'll have passed the first test of a true trapper," suggested Barney as they twisted and turned to find comfortable sleeping positions on their bed of boughs.

As the morning rays of the mid-September sun peeked above the spruce trees on the eastern ridge of the Skeena Mountains, Louie was busy collecting dry firewood for the trappers' anticipated breakfast of Dolly Varden trout. That task completed, he began cutting green alder branches into two-foot lengths. With these he wove a crude grid upon which the trout would be laid as they basted over the hot coals. Meanwhile, Barney had set out for the pool behind a beaver dam just a hundred feet below their evening's campsite. After twenty minutes he returned, holding his catch on the forked branch of a swamp willow.

"Look at these," exclaimed Barney as he deposited eight beautiful fat trout onto the grass beyond the stone floor of the cliff. "Each time I put a grasshopper on my hook and tossed it into the pool a dozen trout tried to grab it. The water behind the dam is filled with trout, all about sixteen to eighteen inches long."

"Boy, they look great!" remarked Louie. "Are you sure eight will be enough?"

"If we can finish these, it will take only a few minutes to catch more, but we have four pounds of fish for each of us, and I think that will be plenty," suggested Barney, who was beginning to look a bit worried. He had once seen Louie devour a twenty-ounce steak as though it was a hamburger, and now he hoped that his estimate of Louie's appetite would not send him back to the stream for more trout.

The glowing coals soon reduced the colorful trout to rusty-colored morsels, recognizable as fish only by their shrunken heads, withered tails, and the aroma of frying fish oil as it spattered over the red hot coals. Without any formality, the famished men retrieved the broiled trout from the bed of steaming alders, peeled away the skin, and literally sucked the delicious flesh from the bony skeletons.

"Man, I could eat trout like this seven days a week," exclaimed Louie as he secured his fourth fish from the simmering twigs. "Barney, you look like you've had enough. Mind if I have the one that's left?"

"Go ahead," offered Barney. "I like trout, too, but not as a steady diet. I need red meat. This reminds me that sometime soon we'll have to lay aside some venison and moose meat. We can catch trout whenever we want, even through the ice, so you can have all the fish you want. However, if we stick to your plan of a long trapline you'll have to catch them for yourself from now on," reminded Barney, who still was not convinced that Louie's proposed three-day circuit was a good idea.

After packing their supplies the two trappers resumed their investigation of the hills and valleys to the north of their cabin.

"OK," announced Louie. "You told me yesterday that you were going to show me how an experienced trapper sets his traps."

Barney, discerning Louie's request to be an admission of inexperience, assumed the role of teacher, foregoing the banter that generally accompanied a confession or discovery of inadequacy by one or the other. "Well, I think if we set traps anywhere on land we should use cubbies," he said.

"Cubbies?" questioned Louie. "What are cubbies?"

"Cubbies are shelters that cover the entire set," explained Barney. "They serve four purposes. First, they protect the trap and the bait from snow, so the trap will always be ready to catch animals. Second, cubbies keep the bait hidden from above so that hawks and eagles won't find it and get caught in our traps. Third, cubbies direct the animal to the bait from a direction that we determine, making it easier for us to place our traps, and fourth, the cubbies will be easier for us to spot when the snow is knee deep. If we build the cubbies right, they'll be high enough so snow won't be a problem."

"Good idea," remarked Louie, resorting to a phrase he used when he was astounded by what he had just heard. "Now show me how to build them and where to place them?"

Convinced that Louie was a complete novice at trapping, Barney took the opportunity to explain in great detail how to build cubbies with the materials at hand in such a way that they would be snow-proof and sturdy. After completing a cubby from the stones, branches, and grasses that were onsite Barney observed, "These cubbies won't stand up under an attack by a wolverine or a bear, but small animals like foxes and fishers will not be able to tear them apart without setting off the trap. Smaller animals will usually go to the bait in the most direct way."

"What about coyotes and wolves?" asked Louie. "There sure are plenty around, judging from the yipping and howling we hear every night."

"Wolves and coyotes won't bother the cubbies unless they are very hungry. If the snow gets deep they may give us trouble, but by that time I hope we're out of here, safe and warm in Prince Rupert."

"What about the winter bear the ole bartender was telling us about?" asked Louie.

"I asked Mackenzie about that story, and he said it was a possibility. Scott said that if a winter bear happened into our trapline we would have to stop everything and kill it. Otherwise, it would just follow our tracks and keep raiding our bait. Let's hope that all the bears in this area are smart enough to hibernate."

Satisfied that Louie understood the techniques of building cubbies and setting traps on high ground, the two trappers began marking potential places where the traps should be set. Their blazes on the aspen and Sitka spruce trees soon reached the quota of traps they intended to set in the woods surrounding the valley. "Foxes will follow trails and will almost always explore a newly dug hole," observed Barney. "So any narrow trail or newly dug hole is a good place to set a trap. See these trails? They are made by raccoons, mink, and weasels, which use them to get to the water. Any trap set in a narrow place along a trail like this will catch an animal. Be sure to pound the stake that holds the trap's chain down to ground level and off the trail so it can't be seen before the animal sees our bait."

As the trappers continued to explore their domain, Barney kept up a continual tutorial for the inexperienced Louie's benefit. "Wear your rubber gloves whenever you touch the traps, and make sure the animal has only one way to get at the bait. Up here, we'll use the no. 1.5 traps to begin with. If we find that fishers and wolverines are setting off the traps and stealing our bait, we'll have to switch to no. 2's. I hope there are not many wolverines in the area. They use a large circuit, maybe forty miles or more, so even if one comes through he generally won't stay more than a day. Fishers can be a real problem because their territory is much smaller. One thing in our favor—they're easy to catch because they're curious. See these tracks? They were made by a male fisher, and a large one at that. We can catch him by building a cubby right against the trunk of that big oak. He loves squirrels, so he'll check the tree to see if there is one in that hole near the top of the trunk."

"Fishers and wolverines aren't nearly as wary of our scent as the mink and martens," continued Barney, "but I think we should boil our traps in tamarack bark when we get to the cabin. That will keep our scent off the traps. These animals don't know human scent yet, but they will soon learn to avoid it if they see the carcasses around with our smells on them."

Although Barney was not convinced that Louie understood all that was required of a successful trapper, he realized that the press of time demanded that experience must now become Louie's primary teacher. The rapid approach of winter had placed the trappers in a situation where knowledge of animal behavior and a sixth sense of how to survive in the wild were much more important ingredients for success than the qualities of unusual strength and endurance. Attributes that had made Louie such a valuable partner during the building of the cabin now faded in importance to his learning to think like the animals they were trying to catch. Barney's plan for the three-day circuit was for Louie to follow him by one day, thereby leaving Barney to harvest the catch of two days, while Louie would retrieve the animals caught in traps that Barney had tended the previous day.

Barney's apprehension about Louie's aptitude as a trapper was short-lived. Ever the practical one, he reasoned that there was nothing further to be done other than to provide as much education and experience as the next few days would permit and then depend on Louie's intelligence and eagerness to do the best possible job. Satisfied that nothing further could be gained by spending more time in the high country, Barney led the way to the marshes and pools surrounding the creeks that flowed into the Skeena River.

Donning their hip boots, Barney and Louie began investigating their prospects among the beaver dams, muskrat lodges, otter slides, and small pools near the river. To an experienced eye, it was easy to see where raccoons and mink had sought frogs and crayfish in the shallow waters. Slides used by otters abounded along the banks of the streams. So numerous were the potential locations for sets that both men were seduced into wishing that Scott Mackenzie had recommended that they bring twice as many traps. "Don't set more traps than you can tend," had been his sage advice. "If you set more than you can tend, the animals will suffer and the pelts will spoil. If not tended everyday, bigger predators will rob your traps and all your work will be wasted." Barney was aware that their three-day circuit would have displeased Scott, but the evidence of fur bearing animals everywhere caused him to disregard the Mounties's advice.

Each man had purchased sufficient traps for a full day of supervision, given that the yield would be as plentiful as Mackenzie had forecast. The euphoria that gripped Barney and Louie at first sight of the bounty that awaited them was soon brought to reality when both realized that an extensive harvest along the river would only hasten the time when the line would have to be extended even further than currently anticipated.

"See this?" questioned Barney as he pointed to the trough entering the stream from a stand of alders. "These cuttings were made by a large, male beaver."

"How do you know that?" asked Louie.

"Because the females and kits won't go this far from the lodge," answered Barney, pointing to a large lodge three hundred feet upriver. "We don't want to set our traps next to the lodge, as tempting as that may be. If we do, we will catch the females and kits and we only want to catch the big males. Remember, if we catch two large beavers from one den, stop trapping in that area. It is important to keep a record of the number and kind of beaver taken from each lodge. Besides, the small ones take nearly as much time to flesh out as the large ones, and their pelts are only worth half as much. Each time you take a beaver near a lodge be sure to place a notch on the tree so we know when we've caught our limit in that area."

Barney then proceeded to show Louie how to place a water-set so that the beaver would be caught by its front feet, dive to the bottom of the pond, and drown within a minute. This method of humane trapping was accomplished by leaving a one-way, forked branch near the bottom of the aspen pole that was used to anchor the trap. "Once the ring that holds the trap passes over the forked branch it will be impossible for the beaver to return to the surface. Always be sure to anchor the pole in at least four feet of water," advised Barney. "Less than that and the beaver will swim to the surface. A beaver's instinct tells him to dive when he's in trouble, and if the anchor is set properly, he will quickly drown. Be sure the anchor pole is pounded down so that it can't be pulled out by a large beaver."

By the end of their second day of exploration, the trappers had determined the perimeter of their trapline. That evening their newly built cabin was the scene of activity long after the sun had disappeared below the horizon. Boards left over from building the cabin were sawed and shaped into fleshing boards. Pelt stretchers and gambrels were sawed and shaped to accommodate the various animal furs. Traps were rotated in and out of a kettle filled with scent destroying tamarack bark. Message caches were built by candle light, each containing sheets of white birch bark, to be used as a primitive communication system.

Long after the candles had been extinguished the two trappers, Barney in the upper bunk and Louie in the lower one, talked about the adventures which lay before them. Neither, in his optimism, dared contemplate the many adversities that might befall them, despite Scott Mackenzie's warnings that the dangers of the northern wilderness were many and most often not subject to prediction. Each fleeting suggestion of danger was dismissed by the self-reliance that could only be attributed to men who were confident that their physical strength and mental toughness would be sufficient to overcome all obstacles. The retreating sliver of moonlight on the cabin floor was the only reminder that the night was far spent. The new challenges before them were only hours away.

September 17 marked the beginning of Barney and Louie's adventure as trappers on their homesteads. After a breakfast of powdered eggs, left-over partridge and bannock the two trappers readied their packs for the three-day excursion on the trapline. Barney, who would precede Louie by one day, kept a watchful eye on Louie's decisions as he packed his supplies for the two-nights in the outposts. He knew that he should have accompanied Louie the first time around the circuit, but the press of time and the desire to have the traps attended as often as possible influenced his judgment to strike out alone and let Louie fend for himself.

The excitement of starting their trapping experience masked the significance of the goodbye and good luck parting words they exchanged that morning. Both were aware that if their plans became reality this would be their last verbal contact for the next three months.

After Barney had detected Louie's inexperience as a trapper during the previous day's outing, both men agreed that Barney should decide where the traps were to be set throughout the entire circuit. By leaving one day ahead of Louie he would determine the location and the length of the trapline. Each trapper would have the option of changing the location of traps as conditions demanded, so long at the decisions were accompanied by carefully marking the newly set traps. As Barney began the task of setting twenty traps along the numerous creeks leading into the Skenna River, he found that opportunities were so numerous he had to remind himself that his sets should be distributed at intervals throughout the entire line between the cabin and the first outpost.

That evening as he cleared away the underbrush and rocks for their first outpost on a dry spot above the river he was aware that all his traps were within several miles from their cabin. If he could find suitable places to set the remaining forty traps in such a close circuit, the work required to maintain the line would be greatly reduced. With this in mind, he set about cutting and stacking a supply of wood so it would be available when the snow covered the deadfalls from which he harvested the dry fuel.

Barney completed the second and third phases of the trapping circuit, overjoyed at the abundant signs of fur in the territory. The second and third phases extended beyond the borders of their homesteads, but well within the capabilities of the men to visit the traps and care for the anticipated catch within the allotted eight hours of daylight available to them. Having completed the three-day circuit Barney, now snug in the cabin, was eager to learn how his Wisconsin style of setting traps would succeed in the Canadian wilderness. Louie, who was to follow Barney the next day, was now two days along the route and would already know the answer.

Louie was filled with excitement as he closed the cabin door and started toward the river, ready to inspect the traps that Barney had set the previous day. To his delight, most of the sets held beaver, otter, or mink, or the traps had been sprung, with the bait missing. Several of the sets held muskrats, which Barney had instructed him to use as bait because of the low price for their fur. Louie tried to reset the traps just as Barney had taught him, but he soon realized that setting a trap in four feet of water without springing the trap required expertise that did not come naturally to him.

After inspecting the twenty traps, easily visible by the blazes Barney had left on the trees, Louie moved to the high ground where both men agreed they would construct the first outpost. Tired from his attempts to replace the water sets, Louie was now faced with skinning the three beaver, one otter, and two mink. He wished that Barney was there to provide firsthand experience in skinning the animals instead of trying to remember how Barney explained the dry-run skinning procedure. He was thankful for the boards that Barney had left at the outpost when it came time to scrape the flesh and fat off the skins. Louie's great strength and skill with an awl served him well during this, the most disagreeable part of the trapping venture. He also learned that skinning animals by the light of a campfire was a difficult task for an inexperienced trapper.

Catching animals proved to be easier than either trapper had anticipated, either because the animals were plentiful, or because the trappers were experts at outwitting the fur bearers. As Barney inspected the accumulating furs in the cache, he was pleased to see that Louie was doing an excellent job of cleaning and drying the furs. Mindful that the high proportion of beaver furs among the total catch would not continue once the ponds, streams, and river froze, Barney was, nevertheless, satisfied that they were well on the way of making a fortune from the anticipated four-month venture. Thus far the three-day circuit was working to perfection.

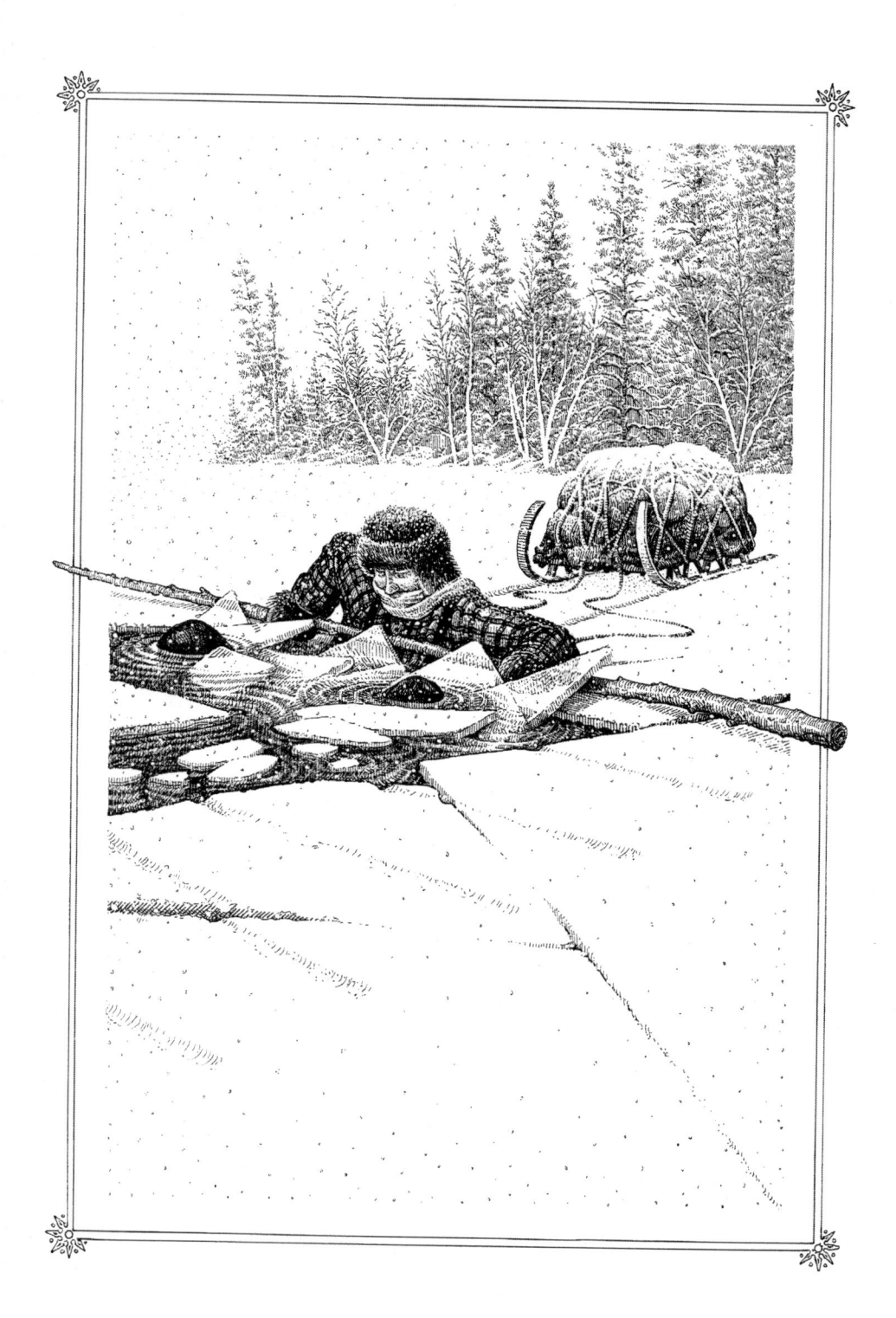

Chapter 7

An Icy Bath in October

As the sun slipped behind the ridge of spruce trees that marked the western edge of the Skenna Mountains a solitary figure stirred beneath the overhanging branches of a large juniper tree. Then it rose and stretched its haunches, extending first one and then the other of its powerful hind legs. Lobo, a huge wolf, had decided it was time for the evening's hunt. He pointed his long, black muzzle to the sky and emitted a sound that at first resembled a low, whining, wail that grew stronger in volume and intensity, forcing the hair on his back to bristle as he ended the call. Ooooo-oooh, ooooo-oooh, swept across the Skeena Valley as Lobo announced to members of the pack that it was time to hunt.

On the opposite side of the valley the call was heard by members of Lobo's pack, which included five mature females, three yearling males, and three pups. Driven by encounters that had often meant the difference between starvation and survival, each member of the pack responded instantly. There was no questioning the authority of Lobo, for it was he upon whom the pack depended for its daily routine. In the last three years Lobo had made the decisions that had increased the size of the pack from a struggling group of three half-starved canines to its present size of a healthy, well-fed family. Once Lobo had emerged as its leader, the pack had seldom gone hungry because their hunts were nearly always successful.

Across the lake that nestled below the hill from which Lobo sounded the call for the evening's hunt a lone figure emerged from the canopy of cedar trees. Exhausted from the day's activities, Barney paused as he, too, heard Lobo's call. Experience told him immediately what the call meant and who had made it. Three weeks in British Columbia's vast wilderness had taught him that Lobo's wolf pack was a well-organized hunting machine. The hills and valleys bordering the Skenna River abounded with large and small animals, so Barney was not surprised by the numerous skeletons of deer and moose that littered the valley that lay within the limits of Lobo's domain-a grim testimony to the efficiency of the resident wolf pack.

The hair on Barney's neck rose momentarily in fear and then anger as Lobo's call drifted across the valley-fear that any movement of the pack toward common ground would surely send them across his tracks-and anger for allowing himself to be seduced by partner Louie Miller's suggestion that they extend their trapline far beyond the legal boundaries of their combined homesteads. Barney had spent an additional hour that day following the stream that led to beaver dams that Louie the previous day had arbitrarily included in their trapline. As a result, Barney was late in achieving his destination—the safety of the cabin with the day's catch of three beaver, two mink, and a pine marten.

The possibility that the wolf pack may have already scented the dead animals on his sled was not lost on Barney as he pondered his predicament. With only minutes of daylight remaining and an additional two miles to travel via shoreline, he knew that it would take him more than an hour to reach the cabin with his heavy load. However, traveling directly across the lake would reduce the distance to one-half mile and bring him home in half an hour.

The words of Mountie Mackenzie rang in Barney's ears as he contemplated his chances of traveling safely across the newly frozen lake. "A pack of hungry wolves will just as soon eat a man as a moose if they can catch you without shelter," had been Mountie Mackenzie warning to the two trappers. "Don't get caught in the woods after dark without shelter and a fire." Mindful that indecision would only compound his problem, Barney made what would soon become a regrettable choice. Almost by second nature, he decided to cross the lake that lay between him and his cabin, knowing full well that the ice had been forming for only one week and may be perilously thin.

Barney hastily unsheathed his hand ax and with swift, sure strokes cut a sapling cedar to use as a supporting crossbar in the event that the ice should break. Holding the cedar pole in one hand and using the other to pull his sled, Barney strode carefully onto the ice. The weak ice creaked and groaned and sent cracks running in all directions, but to Barney's relief he was able to skate slowly across the surface. Then suddenly the groaning ceased, and Barney found himself up to his armpits in the freezing water. The fourteen feet of cedar crossbar kept Barney for being totally immersed in the icy water. By clinging to the crossbar with one hand and using the other to push down lightly against the thin ice, Barney was able to keep his head and shoulders above water as he turned to the shore from which he had just departed.

Years of living on the edge of danger now came to Barney's rescue. Being in precarious situations had prepared him for just this kind of predicament. Quickly, as is the custom of individuals whose lives have included a great number of risk-taking behaviors, he assessed his situation. His sled and its load were intact, although the forward momentum of the sled had stopped it within a foot of the gaping hole in the ice. His .30 Remington semiautomatic rifle, which he carried on a sling, was in place across his shoulder and his backpack in which he carried traps and supplies, although now submerged in water, was secured by two straps that passed over his shoulders and under his armpits.

With the assurance that had accrued from years of fending for himself, Barney turned toward the shore and slowly moved across the large hole toward the sled. Carefully shoving the sled ahead of him, he was able to move through the freezing water at a pace that resembled a slow crawl stroke. The ice surrounding him broke with every forward thrust of his arms, but Barney was able to use the crossbar to keep the sled sufficiently far ahead of the breaking ice. In this manner he moved himself and the sled to within one hundred yards of shore, where to his relief, his feet touched the lake bottom. Although the sled and furs were not yet out of danger from the cracking ice, Barney knew that the first phase of the rescue process had been successful. He would be able to get to shore safely if the icy water did not paralyze him first.

Barney had now been submerged in the freezing water for fifteen minutes. He knew from the shaking of his body and the tremendous chattering of his teeth that hypothermia was only minutes away. Once on shore he quickly stripped the hanging bark off a white birch tree and then gathered an armful of dead branches from the abundant cedar trees that lined the shore. His backpack yielded a tin of waterproof matches, designed for just such an emergency. By now his fingers were devoid of sensation, but the will to survive overcame the messages of surrender that his exhausted body was sending to his brain. The lid on the can of matches yielded to his desperate attempts, with the result that all the matches spilled onto the snow beside his kindling materials. Finally securing one of the priceless incendiaries, he rubbed it forcefully against a dry cedar branch. To his relief, the paraffin gave way and the sulfur head of the match burst into flame. The birch bark and the dry cedar needles quickly responded to the flame, igniting the dry twigs. Soon a crackling fire lighted the forest floor beneath the tall cedars.

When Barney's hands were sufficiently warm, he used the long-handled ax that he carried on his sled to gather a supply of dry wood from the numerous windfalls in the area. With an amply supply of wood on hand and a roaring fire to illuminate his activities, he turned to his physical needs. He knew that any additional attempts to reach the cabin that evening would be foolish, so he resigned himself to spending the night at his present location. His keen hearing told him that he need no longer fear the wolf pack. Their far off call on the trail of some unfortunate beast told him that tonight nature had intervened to spare his life, despite his reckless endeavor to tempt her. He vowed that this close encounter with death would remain in the forefront of his memory during the remainder of his stay in the wilderness. Henceforth, ice-covered lakes would receive greater respect from him.

Replenishing the roaring fire, Barney removed his jacket, shirt, and woolen trousers, which despite his activities, were frozen stiff except where movement at the elbows and knees had sloughed off the brittle sheet of ice. Using forked sticks and rope which he carried in his knapsack, he constructed a clothesline upon which he deposited his outer garments. Experience had taught him that his under garments would dry faster if he wore them and used the combined heat of the fire and that generated by his body to evaporate the water that saturated his underwear and socks. Steam soon rose from the suspended garments and boots, attesting to the efficiency of the roaring fire.

By the time the October moon flooded the lake, which earlier that evening had so nearly ended Barney's dream of freedom and riches in the wilderness, he had stacked a supply of firewood sufficient to last through the night. He now turned his attention to weaving the lower branches of a white spruce tree into a mattress that would serve as his bed that evening. Next he propped each of the animals into a position where the fire would thaw them sufficiently for skinning, but not too close to singe the ends of their beautiful, soft fur.

By nine o'clock the furs, carefully stretched and hanging from their frames, were swaying gently from a line that was tied between two trees. Tomorrow he would place them in the cache with the rest of the season's catch, with never a thought to the circumstances that had so nearly sent them to the bottom of the lake instead off to some furrier and their final destination in the form of coats and hats for Europe's upper class.

As the full moon cleared the tops of the giant cedars only the crackling of the fire and the hoooot, hooot, hooot of a snowy owl broke the stillness. Near the fire, under a large cedar windfall from which the branches facing the fire had been trimmed, slept a fatigued trapper, wrapped in his Hudson Bay blanket. He awakened as if by instinct whenever the fire dwindled into bright, glowing embers. Each replenishment of wood permitted two hours of additional sleep.

The excitement of life in the wilderness and a genetic aversion to sleep found Barney ready for the next day's activities long before daylight. When the sun finally warmed the boughs of the cedars that had served as a blanket to retain the heat of his fire, he was ready to complete the journey that had been so precariously interrupted last evening. As he resumed his trek to the cabin he glanced once more at the blue ice that marked the spot near the middle of the lake where his great adventure had nearly come to a premature end. With a shrug of his shoulders he turned away from the scene, unmindful that it would be the first of many experiences to test his remarkable endurance, his knowledge of the wilderness, and his ability to overcome whatever predicaments he encountered because of his risk-taking personality.

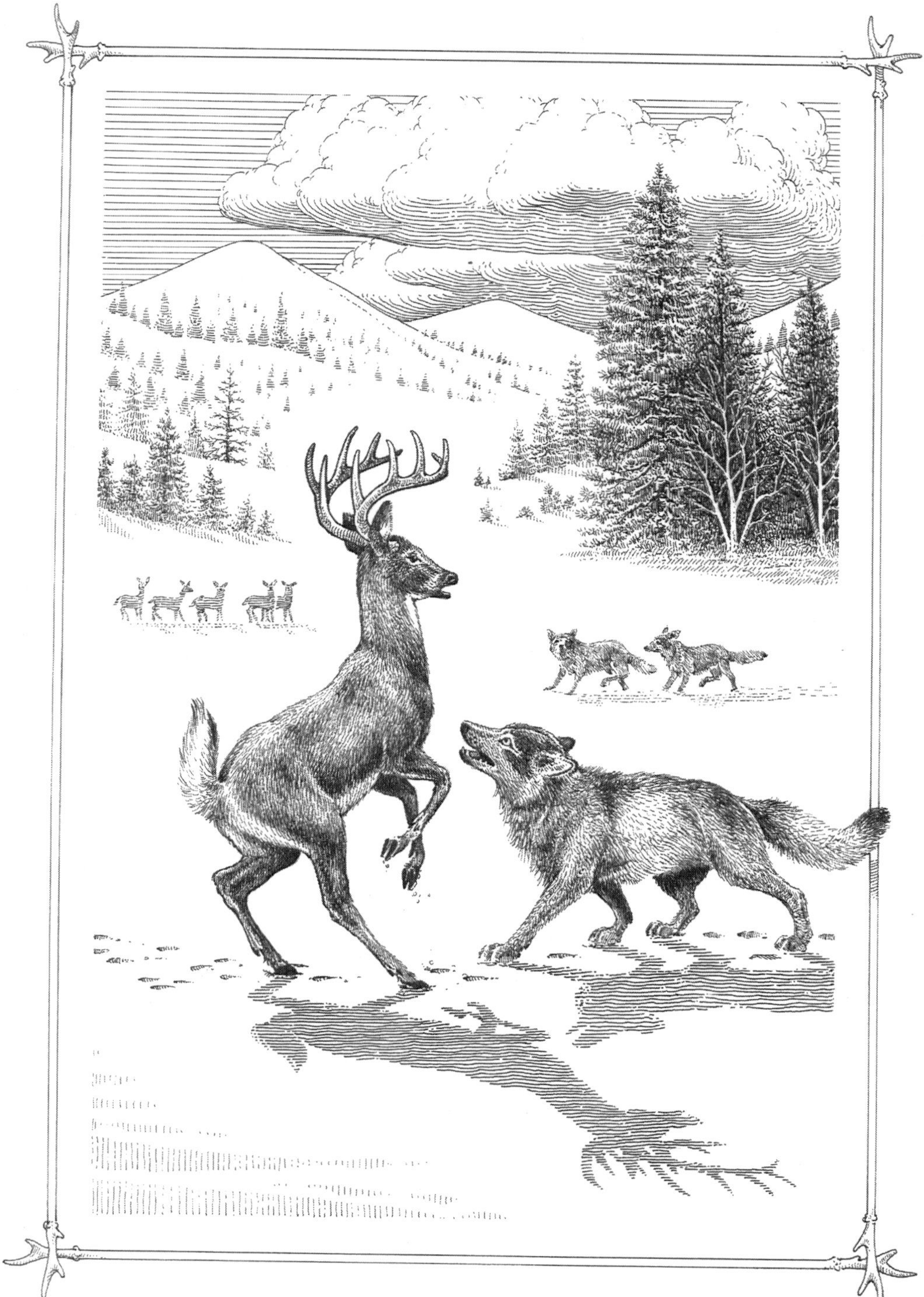

Chapter 8

Adventures with Wolves

Cannibalism among wolves

The heavy sled came to an abrupt halt as Barney stopped at the fire pit adjacent to the lean-to that would be his shelter for the evening. He had chosen to use his sled to haul his supplies even though there were still places of insufficient snow, which caused the sled to scrape on the rocks and grass along the trail. As Barney visited the twenty traps that were set along the second part of their three-day circuit he was amazed and pleased at the abundance of furs that Louie and he continued to harvest. He actually looked forward to the long hours required each evening to properly prepare the pelts for stretching and drying.

As he plucked the feathers from the two ptarmigan that he had shot just an hour ago his mouth watered at the thought of roasted foul, twisting on an alder stick, after having subsisted on trout and venison for the past several days.

As the depth of the November snow increased, Barney had become increasingly annoyed at the defiance of the resident wolf pack, which recently had begun to follow him along the trapline to his campsite. During the last two nights he had been kept awake by the howling, snapping, and fighting among the members of the pack as they devoured their victims, usually a moose, deer, or caribou. Tonight he would teach them a lesson.

After skinning the three beavers and two mink which constituted his catch that day, Barney chambered a round into his .30 Remington, placed the sling over his shoulder, and picked up the carcasses of the animals. Approximately seventy-five yards from his campsite he stopped beside three small aspen trees and hung the carcasses in branches approximately seven feet from the ground. Retreating to his campfire, he sat on a log with his rifle across his lap and sipped his standard cup of tea.

As darkness engulfed the woods surrounding the campsite Barney heard Lobo's call, summoning his pack for the evening's hunt. Barney correctly anticipated that the scent of the carcasses hanging in the trees a short distance from his campfire would be detected by Lobo's keen nose. The answering calls of the pack members told Barney that the wolves were on their way to check out the scent of fresh game. Tonight perhaps the pack anticipated a short and effortless hunt.

Soon the barking ceased, but Barney was able to see dark forms lurking in the distance. Flames from his large fire illuminated the open space between him and the bait in the trees. Unable to reach the carcasses, the wolves milled around, attempting to dislodge the bait that hung just beyond their reach. When Barney was satisfied that the entire pack had gathered in a small area he shouldered his rifle and fired at the pair of gleaming green eyes nearest him. The thud of the bullet and the yelp of the victim told him that his bullet had found its mark.

What happened next reinforced Barney's contention that wolves were among the lowest form of predators existing in the Canadian wilderness. The intense snarling, growling, and fighting told Barney that the wolves had turned on their own kind. Apparently the smell of blood was so overpowering that members of their own pack, if wounded, were subject to the same kind of vicious attack that wolves inflicted on their prey.

Inspection of the scene the next morning confirmed Barney's belief that the wolves had engaged in cannibalistic behavior the previous evening. The snow beneath the aspen trees where the bait still hung was packed down from the fighting that had taken place. Here and there Barney found tufts of hair and skin that had so recently belonged to one of their pack mates—perhaps to a sister, brother, or mother. A pool of blood on the fresh snow indicated where Barney's shot had found its mark, but the carcass of the victim, including most of the hide and the entire skeleton, had been devoured. Barney shuddered at the thought of being confronted in the woods without adequate defenses by a pack such as the one that had visited his campfire the previous evening. He vowed that wolves would never have an opportunity to exert their savagery on him.

Lobo shows his strength

When Louie and Barney designed the three-day circuit of their trapline they had purposefully intended the third portion of the route to be shorter than the rest, thus allowing sufficient time for the trapper to properly store his furs, cook a nutritious meal, and do his laundry-tasks that were not easily accomplished at the two outpost sites. Barney relished the time he could spend in the cabin because of the comfort the shelter provided from the cold and blowing snow. Lately he had become accustomed to climbing the fifteen-foot ladder that led to the fur cache, using the elevated seat to survey the lake and hills beyond the cabin. His powerful binoculars enabled him to study the wildlife that seemed to use the hours just before dusk as its preferred time to seek water and food.

Tonight, as he scanned the shore across the lake, he was rewarded by the sight of a large white-tailed buck that had come to the water's edge to drink. Suddenly the buck raised his head as though startled by something in the bushes behind him. His keen sense did not deceive him because within minutes Lobo appeared and immediately approached the buck. The buck took up the challenge. With head lowered, he chased Lobo around the open space on the lake shore. The buck's massive horns were more than a match for Lobo, who managed to stay just out of reach from each vicious charge. After approximately ten minutes of this dash-and-evade tactic, Lobo backed away from the buck. Barney assumed that Lobo now realized that the fight provided no contest, and he would leave to seek an easier victim. However, the events that followed gave evidence that Lobo had only enacted the first part of his plan.

As the buck lowered his head, preparing to charge again, perhaps with the thought of chasing Lobo entirely out of the clearing, Lobo pointed his muzzle toward the hillside and gave two short barks, made apparent to Barney by the puffs of steam emitted from his mouth. In another minute two wolves, nearly as large as Lobo, emerged from the cedars. The buck realized immediately that the battle had taken on a new dimension. Before the three wolves could attack he backed into the lake until the water reached his hocks. Perhaps believing that the wolves would not follow him into the water, he waited to see their reaction. He did not have long to wait.

The two wolves that Lobo had summoned ran into the water. As the buck turned to face them, Lobo approached from the rear. Immediately, the buck turned to face Lobo, but as he did so the two wolves attacked his flanks. As the buck was distracted by the two wolves, Lobo saw his chance. He sprang and grabbed the buck's nose, clamping his huge mouth across its upper and lower jaws. The weight of Lobo brought the buck to his knees. The two wolves at the buck's rear now pulled the buck down until his legs gave way under him. At this point Lobo released his hold on the buck's head and grabbed him by the neck, just behind the lower jaw. Within seconds the buck ceased to struggle and the battle was over. Barney had watched the entire contest through his binoculars, aware that he was helpless in his perch four hundred yards away to aid the buck. However, what he saw next reinforced his respect for the power and skill of Lobo.

The lifeless body of the big buck lay in approximately eighteen inches of water. Barney supposed that the three wolves would drag the carcass to the shore and gorge themselves at that spot. However, Lobo had other plans. While his two combat assistants stood and watched, Lobo grabbed the buck by the neck and quickly dragged him twenty feet beyond the water's edge. Then he bit off chunks of fur around the neck of the buck, casting aside the hair and skin that resulted from this procedure. He then turned the buck on its back so its antlers dug into the ground. Next he positioned himself parallel to the buck's body and with quick jerks, removed the entire hide from the buck as though it had been done in a butcher's shop.

When he finished his maneuver the hide of the buck, turned fur side in, lay on the ground next to the denuded animal. The entire process of skinning the buck had taken no longer than five minutes. Barney watched in awe at the tremendous strength of Lobo. The buck, he estimated, weighed over two hundred pounds, yet Lobo had dragged him from the water as if he was a faun. The task of skinning the buck would have taken two men fifteen minutes, even with the use of a block and tackle and a gambrel. Lobo had demonstrated to members of his pack why he was the alpha male.

Lobo's pack kills for joy

Barney emerged from the canopy formed by the cedar trees that marked the end of his trapline. The lake where he had been so unceremoniously immersed a month ago was now frozen, covered with a six-inch layer of ice and several inches of snow. As he approached the lake, which he intended to cross on his way to the cabin, he noted that the higher temperatures of several days ago had thawed the snow, which had now refrozen, resulting in large patches of ice on top of the snow near the middle of the lake. He reminded himself to avoid these areas, having learned that the newly frozen ice may not be safe. Skirting the icy patches, he pulled his sled up the bank and parked it under the overhang of the cabin. He reminded himself that he should first provide a sufficient supply of wood for the stove while there was sufficient light to select oak pieces from the woodpile. He would tend to the animals that he had harvested that day when all the other chores had been addressed.

As Barney turned to the cabin, his arms loaded with wood, he heard a chorus of barks that were unusual in their nearness to the cabin. As he gazed across the lake he could see a herd of deer on the opposite shore. Hurrying to retrieve his binoculars from the sled, he learned that his original observation was correct. Eleven deer were milling about on the shoreline directly across from the cabin. Soon Barney learned why the deer seemed to be in such a state of confusion. Out of the woods, completely surrounding the herd, came the members of Lobo's pack. As the wolves moved forward the deer realized that there was but one avenue of escape. Seeing their retreat to the woods cut off, the deer ran onto the lake, perhaps with the intent of crossing to the other side on a path that would have taken them near the homesteaders' cabin.

Once the deer were on the lake it appeared to Barney that they would be able to outrun the wolves and make their escape. However, Lobo was not about to let the deer have a choice. By moving to their left, he was able to direct them onto the frozen field of ice in the middle of the lake. Once the deer were on the ice their smooth hooves, great for running when traction was good, betrayed them. As they slid and scrambled on the slippery surface Lobo and the members of his pack ran up to one after the other, grasping them by the throat and slashing their jugular veins until all eleven deer lay dead on the icy surface. When the massacre was completed, to Barney's surprise, the wolves trotted off into the woods. None of the wolves made an attempt to eat any of the carcasses.

Barney's life in the wild had taught him that everything in nature occurs for a purpose. At times man had not understood or appreciated these occurrences, but Barney realized that the laws of survival, so deeply ingrained in the lives of animals, had for centuries contributed to the survival and revival of the species. With this rationale in mind, Barney attempted to justify the sadistic actions that he had just seen. Was Lobo teaching the pack how to store food for the future? Was he teaching the younger members of the pack how to hunt? Was this another method of demonstrating Lobo's dominance?

Barney decided to monitor the activities of Lobo's pack in relation to the fallen deer in an attempt to learn the reason for the killings. Week after week he checked the carcasses with his binoculars, but none of the wolves ever returned to feed on the deer. By the end of November the dead deer had become a favorite feeding site for ospreys, eagles, and ravens. Foxes also visited the site, but wolves ignored it. Barney concluded that Lobo's pack had killed simply for the joy of killing. In his long years as a hunter and trapper he had never seen animals, with the exception of wolves, exhibit this form of grotesque behavior.

Hunting strategies of Lobo's pack

Lobo's opening call this evening seemed sharper and more of a bark than his usual howl. Barney noted this departure from normal had also been present for the last several nights. Did the wolves sense some change in their environment? Was the Skeena Valley about to receive the fabled snowstorm that he had been told could stop all movement, including those of moose and wolves, for days? Barney decided to investigate. He grabbed his binoculars, put on his mackinaw jacket, and climbed the ladder to his favorite seat in the doorway of the fur cache.

Far to the north, along the Skeena River, he saw a small group of animals of what at first appeared to be a herd of deer. However, there was something unusual about the way the herd moved. Some animals ran a short distance and then waited for the remainder to catch up, then the process was repeated. Deer, Barney noted, usually ran as a unified group this early in the year. As the animals came more clearly into focus he noted that they were woodland caribou.

As the herd approached, Barney learned why they were running along at this helter-skelter fashion. Trailing behind the herd were three large wolves. The curious part of the drama being played out in front of Barney was that neither the caribou nor the wolves seemed to be in any hurry. The caribou did not seem to regard the wolves as a threat, and the wolves seemed more intent on herding the caribou than in attacking them. When the caribou reached the end of the open shoreline on the opposite side of the lake it became clear why the wolves had dictated such a leisurely pace.

Just as the caribou were about to disappear into the thicker cover of the forest, three other wolves emerged from the cedars in front of the caribou. Seeing the wolves, the caribou halted, then wheeled in the direction from which they had just come. The wolves that initially chased them had disappeared, so the area to the north of the river was clear of enemies. But now the pace increased. The second wave of wolves followed more closely, nipping at the heels of the slowest members of the herd until the herd was running at nearly full speed.

Caribou, built for endurance and modest speed, could outrun wolves without much effort if the contest depended on distance covered over rough terrain. However, the strategy that Lobo had devised allowed the wolves to use their superior speed over short distances, thus creating a contest in which the odds favored the pack. As soon as the second relay of wolves had chased the caribou back approximately one-half mile they stopped the chase and disappeared into the dense woods. To the surprise of the caribou, another group of four wolves appeared before them, again causing them to reverse their direction.

Barney watched with begrudging admiration at the strategy of Lobo. As his pack of relay hunters wore down the confused caribou it was only a matter of time before the tired beasts fell easy victim to the ferocious fangs of Lobo's pack. Once again, the carnage occurred with a savagery that could only be interpreted as killing for the pure joy of killing. When the last caribou had been dispatched the entire pack of wolves returned to the scene of the chase. There the thirsty hunters lapped up the bloodstained snow, but none of the caribou were eaten then or in the days that followed. In the ensuing weeks, as Barney passed the frozen carcasses on his way from the trapline to the cabin, he vowed that in a small way he would avenge the deer and the caribou that had fallen victim to the wolves' love of killing. When the snow became too deep for Lobo's pack to hunt and kill at will Barney would use Lobo's keen sense of smell to lure the big wolf into one of his traps.

Lobo caught and freed

The accumulating snow in the Skeena Valley, now over a foot high, increased the energy that moose, deer, and caribou expended each day to find sufficient food. Lobo's pack, conversely, found it easier to chase down the large animals, whose hooves penetrated the snow and easily tired them in the nightly chases that were a favorite hunting technique of the wolves. The snow became a blueprint for Barney, who studied the behavior of the wolves from the tracks they left along the trappers' route. Until recently wolves had ignored the baited traps, but now Barney noticed that the pack frequently followed the trapline, devouring the carcasses of the skinned animals that the trappers left at the two outposts.

"Put dead animals in trees-away from trapline," had been the message Barney left for Louie, hoping to discourage the increasingly close proximity of wolves' nightly hunts to their trapline. Barney could tell from the tracks that wolves were more frequently following the snowshoe trails that Louie and he used to visit their traps. Sooner or later the wolves would attack the baited cubbies, and more destructively, feast on the animals caught in the traps. Barney understood that the reason such predatory behavior had not yet occurred was because of the discipline that Lobo exercised over his pack. Lobo understood that the traps meant danger. Until hunger drove his pack to such extreme hunting techniques, he would have them chasing the large animals that now seemed more hesitant to run when confronted by the wolf pack.

Barney's observations of the wolves had left him with a grudging admiration for the efficiency with which they carried out their daily hunts. Once on the trial of an animal, the outcome was predictable, signified by the chorus of howls that accompanied the feast after a kill. The intermittent howling while eating apparently was a signal of jubilation, and perhaps a declaration of superiority to other predators, such as coyotes, cougars, and bears.

The two outposts provided an excellent observation point for the evening hunts, which always began with the low, plaintive call by Lobo to his pack. Shortly thereafter the trappers could hear the short, choppy barks of the pack as they pursued whatever game Lobo's keen nose had selected as their prey that evening. The hunts usually lasted less than half an hour, followed by a chorus of howls while the pack feasted. By ten o'clock the valley was usually quiet, except for the yip, yip, yip of coyotes and the hooting of snowy owls.

As the deep snow of November took its toll on victims and victors, alike, the predation of wolves along the trapline became increasingly more frequent. Recent events indicated that Lobo had given his approval for individual pack members to raid the traps, mostly in their late afternoon forays prior to the customary evening hunts. However, Lobo's large prints were never among those at the pilfered sites. If Barney was to catch Lobo it would take extreme cunning. Lobo was not likely to be lured into the usual cubby that the trappers had set for smaller game.

Barney knew that the den used by Lobo and his pack was in the rocky, high ground to the eastern side of their trapline. Lobo's calls to his pack always originated in the east-calls that he used to bring the pack home from their daytime wanderings in the valley.

As Barney was about to enter the protective barrier of fir trees leading to the second outpost he spied a large buck grazing on willow shoots near one of the feeder creeks. In need of meat, Barney shot the buck and placed the hind quarters on his sled, to be taken to the cabin the next day. He cut out the tenderloins, which he intended to broil for his evening meal.

With sufficient daylight to carry out his plan, Barney placed the front quarters of the buck on his sled and pulled it several hundred yards north of his camping site, where he buried the remains of the carcass under snow and brush, leaving a natural opening for animals to access the bait. Next he set three no. 2 traps behind the bait, anticipating that Lobo would not approach the carcass from the front. Carefully concealing the traps in the snow and sweeping the entire area with a broom made from a spruce bough, Barney hoped that the falling snow would be his ally in further hiding whatever evidence he left behind. As he skinned the animals he had removed from traps that day he wondered if hunger would seduce Lobo to visit his lure. The close proximity of the set to Lobo's den was sure to attract the attention of the wolves.

As the morning sun brought daylight to the valley Barney shouldered his pack and headed to the place where he hoped to find Lobo. He knew that something had agitated the wolf pack the previous evening because their customary howling had not occurred.

As Barney approached the site of the hidden buck he could hardly believe his eyes. There, passively lying in the snow, as calmly as if he was on the floor of someone's living room, was Lobo. The big wolf, caught by a hind and a front foot, raised his head and looked at Barney, reminiscent of a dog greeting his master. Absent was the snarling and attempted biting that Barney expected. As Barney drew within five feet and pointed his .22 caliber pistol at Lobo's head, the huge canine seemed ready to accept his fate. With downcast eyes the big wolf looked at Barney's feet, ready to meet his destiny.

Barney surveyed the scene before him and did what no one, including himself, would have predicted. A lifelong lover of dogs, Barney lowered his pistol and placed it in his pack. Next he cut a sapling to use as a protective barrier. He placed the sapling between Lobo and himself as he stepped on the spring of the trap that held Lobo's hind paw. Once freed of the trap, Barney expected Lobo to resort to the aggressive behavior that had made him such a successful hunter, but Lobo continued in his passive posture. Barney knew that attempting to free Lobo's front paw would place him in a precarious position, should Lobo attempt to use his vicious teeth. But the wolf lay quietly as Barney placed the sapling next to Lobo's neck, stepping on the spring to free his front paw. The wolf was now entirely free. With an upward glance at Barney, Lobo pulled himself erect and slowly limped into the underbrush. Just before he disappeared Lobo looked back at Barney as if to express his gratitude. Both the hunter and the hunted had displayed the respect that can only occur when two combative enemies engage in competition. Both knew that in his present condition Lobo's days as leader of the pack were over. From this day onward one of Lobo's sons would sound the call for the evening hunt.

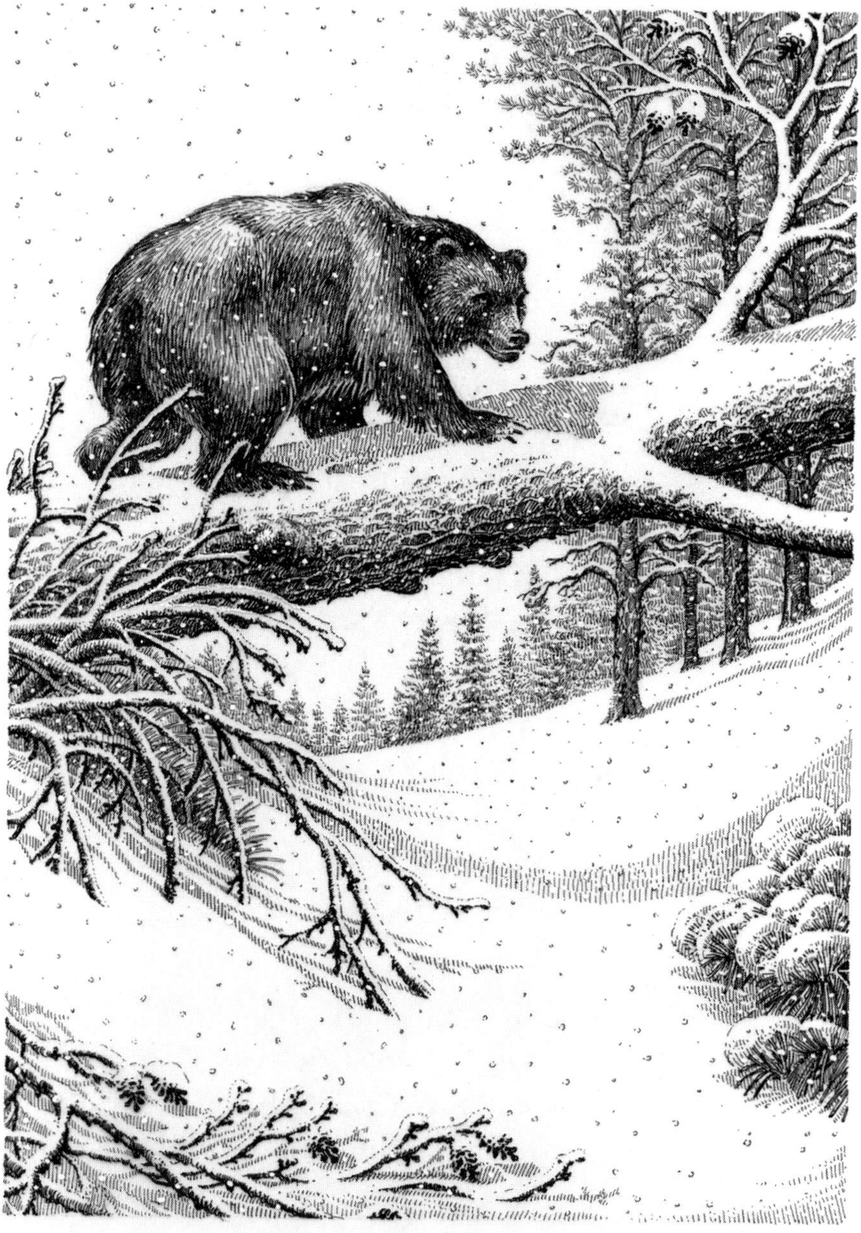

Chapter 9

The Winter Bear

Barney finished his morning cup of tea with an unusual apprehension about the day's activities. He banked the bed of coals that remained from his fire at the trappers' second outpost with a greater than usual heap of ashes to ensure that the insulation would last until Louie reached the site later in the day. The territory between the second and third outposts had been the best fur-producing part of the trapline. Today Barney was anxious to see what the past two days had produced. While still ten strides from the first cubby his face tensed in anger. Rocks and sticks of which the cubby had been constructed were strewn about. More disturbing, tufts of fur that had recently belonged to a trapped mink were scattered in the snow. Tracks in the snow told Barney that a bear had visited the cubby and eaten the victim and the bait that had lured it into the trap. A winter bear, the nemesis of trappers in wilderness areas, had discovered the homesteaders' trapline and the feast that accompanied such a finding. Mountie Mackenzie had mentioned that infrequently a two or three-year-old male grizzly would not hibernate, but forage on whatever food was available throughout the winter, seeking the den of a female, killing her newborn cubs, with the intention of mating with her in the spring.

Barney knew immediately what his discovery of the destroyed cubby meant. Likely the scene before him would be repeated as he traveled north and east along the trapline. Inspection of the next three cubbies confirmed his suspicion. The bear has systematically destroyed the cubbies, eaten the caught animals, or set off the traps and eaten the bait. Barney knew that by now the bear was likely asleep, hiding in the high ground of dense firs that bordered the river. Having eaten his fill, the bear was not likely to continue his predatory behavior until the following evening. However, the trappers could not permit a repeat performance. Barney would have to track the bear to his lair and kill him.

Seething with anger as he inspected each decimated cubby, Barney scouted the area for tracks that would lead him to the bear's resting place. Prudence suggested that he seek Louie's help in dispatching the bear, but self-confidence and expediency had always directed Barney's actions. Barney knew that Louie had elected to carry a shotgun instead of a rifle, revealing to Barney that Louie did not trust his aim as a marksman.

Barney reasoned that perhaps Louie would be more of a liability than an asset in the situation that faced him. In addition, seeking Louie, one day behind Barney, would delay the hunt for a day and perhaps allow the bear to destroy another day's catch. Anger about the unforeseen turn of event overcame whatever fear Barney had for own his well-being as he continued to seek the bear's exit tracks. Several hundred yards along the trapline he found the tracks leading into a stand of Sitka spruce.

Past experience had taught him that predators do not travel far on a full stomach. Barney also knew that the bear was aware of his presence, having been within two hundred yards of his campsite the following evening. The bear's keen sense of smell would surely detect Barney's presence on this quiet morning, so the element of surprise would be lost. With that in mind, Barney chambered a round into the breach of his rifle, checked to ensure that the magazine carried its capacity of five rounds, and set off to find the bear. He placed his index finger on the safety of his .30 Remington semiautomatic, carried the rifle at waist height, and gingerly stepped into the grove of trees. He realized that his medium-caliber rifle was no match for a large grizzly, but the confidence he had in his ability to shoot accurately would have to be the equalizer today. Unless the grizzly caught him totally by surprise Barney would be able to squeeze off all six rounds before the bear reached him.

To Barney's relief the stand of spruce trees surrounded a small meadow. Barney knew if he could get to the meadow before the bear attacked he would have a much better chance of avoiding an ambush. As he entered the west side of the meadow he heard a roar from the far side. The bear, having scented Barney, had been watching to see who had disturbed his rest. Standing erect to better accentuate his poor eyesight, the bear waited to see what his pursuer would do. The warning growl and the erect posture gave Barney the chance he needed to aim and fire at the exposed chest of the grizzly. Two shots found their mark before the grizzly could get on all four feet. As the bear entered the meadow Barney aimed at the up-and-down movement of the head and chest, successfully sending four more bullets into the lumbering beast. Shot after shot found its mark. Even though fatally wounded, the amazing strength and stamina of the big bear propelled him into the middle of the clearing, intent on finding his tormenter. Barney, his magazine now empty, sought hurriedly to reload, but his expert marksmanship had taken its toll. Before he could get an additional round into firing position the bear dropped, having moved to within forty feet of Barney before his charge was halted by loss of blood from the numerous bullets.

As Barney inspected the glossy coat of the young grizzly he realized how fortunate he had been to see the bear at a distance. An older bear would have waited in ambush for Barney to approach instead of announcing its presence and then crossing the meadow in pursuit of its quarry. Barney was overjoyed at the morning's triumph, confident that he had made the right decision in pursuing the bear on his own. Once again, luck and his great marksmanship had extracted him from a potentially dangerous situation into which he had thrust himself by making a decision without regard for his personal safety.

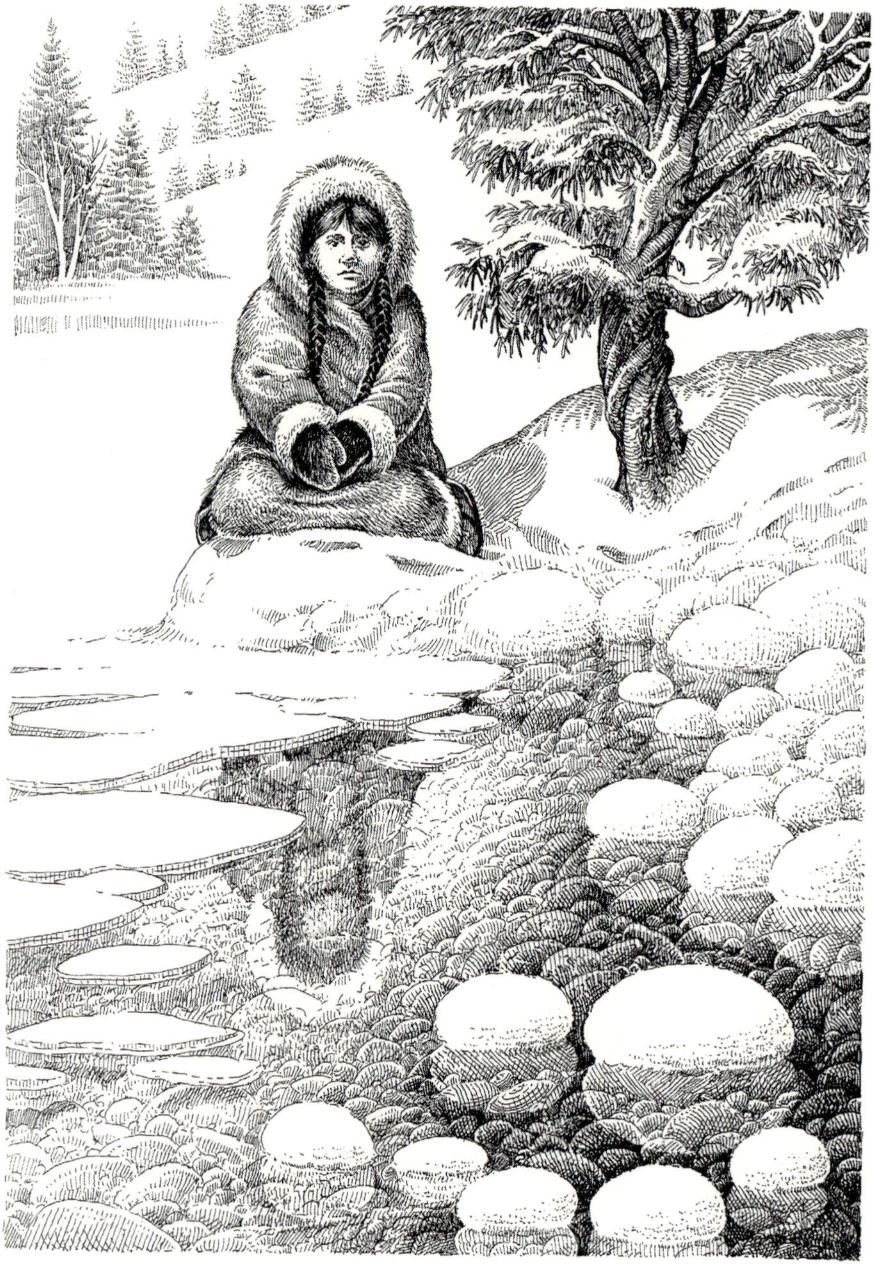

Chapter 10

Metonka Flees Her People

    Metonka raised her head slightly, peering out from her cover of moose and caribou hides at the two forms sleeping on the tent floor. The two women who shared the tent with her that night were Grey Eagle's other wives, both older than Metonka. As per the custom, the older wives were Metonka's superiors regarding any work that was to be done around the camp. Although Grey Eagle had initially shown that Metonka was his favorite wife, lately he had grown cross and abusive to her. Metonka was now fifteen years old, with long, black hair and a beautiful, willowy body to match the features of her lovely face.

    As was the custom among the Indians of the subarctic tribes, the most powerful man in the village, always the chief, was able to dictate whatever happened in the village, including the selection and assignment of marriages among the men and women. When Metonka was fourteen Grey Eagle had announced to her father, Tesuema, that he wished to take Metonka for his third wife. Tesuema, now old and feeble, had neither the strength nor the will to resist such a pronouncement, although in his heart he knew that Grey Eagle did not represent the trustworthy, honest warriors who had preceded him as chief of his proud band.

Metonka's people were one of the many small bands that roamed in the Yukon and Northern British Columbia. As nomads, they followed the salmon and caribou-their chief sources of food. Their houses were dome-shaped, constructed of poles covered with caribou hides. The floors were covered with furs except for a space in the center where a stone-lined fire was kept burning by the women. A smoke hole near the top of the dome kept most of the smoke out of the hogan. Meals were cooked outside, over a large fire, which was tended by the women. Encampments were always near a river, lake, or steam.

Metonka was very angry with her father for agreeing to Grey Eagle's demands that she marry him. Her heart belonged to Blue Cloud, a handsome, strong half-brother of Grey Eagle who was the son of Red Feather's second wife. However, Blue Cloud was only eighteen and no match for Grey Eagle when it came to fighting or even leading the men on their annual hunting trips. Someday, Metonka knew, Blue Cloud would challenge Grey Eagle for the leadership of the tribe, but that challenge was several years away. Reluctantly, she had gone to Grey Eagle's lodge because there was no other course of action available to her. If she wished to stay with her people she would have to obey Grey Eagle.

Metonka had enjoyed a happy childhood. Each summer the people of her village moved close to Fort Babine by following the Sheena River south to it's junction with the Babine River, where she had spent her girlhood playing with the white children, offspring of the fur traders and military men who occupied the combined Fort and Trading Post and the Métis children, offspring of the trappers who had taken Indian wives. Through her association with the children who lived in the trading post she had learned of the white men's customs and knew how to speak "broken English."

More recently Metonka had come to admire the way the white men treated their wives and children. She knew that Indian wives of the white men sat at the table and ate with the men and their children. In her village the men were served first and ate the best of the meat and fish. The women and children ate only when the men had eaten their full, which in times of hardship often left little for the hungry mouths that far outnumbered those of the men. She also knew that the white men seldom, if ever, beat their wives, but in her village it was common for women to be beaten whenever the husbands became angry. Often the cause of the anger had nothing to do with domestic relationships, but the wives received the abuse, nevertheless.

Some time ago Metonka had decided that she would not tolerate anymore physical abuse from Grey Eagle. She had waited until now, when Grey Eagle's men were on their fall hunting trip, to carry out her plan to escape from a life that she could no longer tolerate. As was Grey Eagle's custom when his men were on their hunting trips, that evening he had consumed great portions of the fire water that had been given to him by the white traders in exchange for furs, many of which she had trapped herself. She knew that Grey Eagle would sleep until noon, after a night of drinking the fire water. When he awoke he would be demanding and mean. Woe be it to any of his wives who did not serve him as he directed. Tomorrow, Metonka vowed, the punishment would befall his other wives, for Metonka's plan was to be far from the village by then.

Despite Metonka's stirrings, the other wives continued their deep sleep. With her razor sharp awl she cut the strands of moose sinew that held together the large pieces of caribou hide from which the tent was made. The small opening near the bottom of the tent through which Metonka squeezed her graceful body would not be noticed by the wives. Ultimately, Metonka's absence would be attributed to an early excursion into the woods to trap ptarmigan, which was also a familiar routine of hers. She hoped that she would not be missed until noon of the next day.

As soon as Metonka emerged from the tent she reached into a woven bag suspended from a shoulder strap from which she extracted fish scraps that she had placed there the previous evening. She knew that is was important to silence the dogs, whose barking and whining at this late hour would be sure to arouse suspicion. Once she had fed the dogs she laced her snowshoes to her back and started away from the encampment in a northerly direction.

Metonka knew that as soon as she was missed Grey Eagle would demand that everyone in camp begin to search for her. Metonka wanted the campers to believe that she had gone to her grandmother's village, some sixty miles to the north, which was exactly opposite from the direction that she intended to take. She intentionally stepped into the new fallen snow without her snowshoes so the tracks would be visible for a longer time. Once beyond the encampment she donned her snowshoes with the hope that the drifting snow would cover the imprints and hide her change of direction to the south.

Metonka had listened with great interest as the fur traders at Fort Babine spoke of the great city to the southwest, which they called Prince Rupert. They told tales of a city that was visited by great ships that came to the harbor from other parts of the land far beyond her home. The city was also home of a great iron horse that moved on wheels. The fur traders speculated that it was only a matter of time before the iron horse reached Fort Babine, but

Metonka was not prepared to wait. Today she was going to set out for the big city or die in her attempt to do so.

She had no idea how long it would take her to get to Prince Rupert, but her bag carried flint and steel for fires, some venison jerky for nourishment while she walked, an extra pair of moccasins and some snares for catching ptarmigan and rabbits along the way. Around her waist she carried a dagger that she could use as a knife, hatchet, or ax. Although she had never been this far south she felt perfectly at home in the woods, having lived there most of her young life.

Metonka knew that in a test of endurance she could keep up to the strongest of the warriors because her snowshoes would not sink as far into the snow, allowing her to travel faster and use less energy than the heavier men. She also realized that she must stay ahead of any pursuers or suffer the wrath of Grey Eagle and the rest of the village. As soon as they discovered that she had fled they would look for her with a vengeance. Metonka was determined that by the time they learned of her plan she would be in Prince Rupert. She did not know what she would do once she got there, but she doubted that any of Grey Eagle's warriors would venture into the city. Once in Prince Rupert she hoped that someone would listen to her story and take care of her.

When Metonka reached the forest to the north of the encampment she slipped her moccasin-clad feet into the leather bindings of her snowshoes and set off at a modified run that encircled the encampment in a southerly direction. Her exceptional athletic ability, especially on snowshoes, would permit her to keep up this pace for hours. The full moon provided sufficient light for her to avoid the small stumps and branches that might entangle her snowshoes and cause her to fall. The new snow, still falling lightly, would hide her tracks. With a north wind at her back the tracks would be further obliterated by the time Grey Eagle and his men set out in pursuit.

Metonka traveled in this modified run for several hours along the animal trails that traversed the hills above Grey Eagle's encampment. Then she headed toward the big river, which she knew flowed toward her destination, Prince Rupert. Once on the river she was able to move so rapidly that even the most skillful of men on snowshoes would have had difficulty keeping up to her. After nearly eight hours at such a pace, during which she had taken time only to drink from the handfuls of snow that she scooped up while bending down to avoid low-hanging braches, she decided to rest. Seeking out a large Norway spruce tree with branches that swooped clear to the ground, she crawled under the snow-covered canopy, curled up in her shawl of caribou hides and within minutes was fast asleep.

Metonka awakened with a start. Was that someone approaching, or was it the snow falling in clumps from the branches of her shelter? She peeked through the openings of the low-hanging branches, first up the river and then in all directions as she circled the trunk of the big Norway Spruce tree. She kept up this surveillance for many minutes until she was sure that the noise had not been made by her pursuers. It would be dark in another hour. Then she would continue her journey into country that she believed to be beyond the reach of Grey Eagle. If he had sent one of his men high into the hills to look for her along the river, the approaching darkness would provide the cover she needed. One more ten-hour trek should put sufficient miles between her and any of Grey Eagle's men. Only then would she be able to relax and enjoy her journey to the big city.

When the approaching darkness made it impossible for Metonka to see objects more than a hundred yards away she crept from the cover of her shelter, slid her feet into the bindings of her snowshoes, and headed once again for the river. The moon illuminated the snowbound river, enabling Metonka to resume the characteristic modified run that ate away the miles.

Far in the distance to the south she heard the hunting call of the resident wolf pack. Little did she know that it was Lobo's pack, and that in the days ahead she would become much better acquainted with that mournful sound. Now, for the first time since she began her journey, her thoughts turned to what she would do if confronted on the river by wolves. Indian women were not allowed to use firearms, so she had not learned how to shoot a rifle. Her only weapon was a long-bladed hunting knife that had been her father's. However, the fear of what lay to the north was much greater than any impending attack by wolves, so she dismissed the thought and concentrated on keeping the swish-swish-swish of her snowshoes moving her steadily southward.

By the time the rising sun peeked over the edge of the Babine Range of the Skeena Mountains Metonka had traveled eight hours during her second day of escape. She had eaten nothing but four strips of venison jerky, which she chewed as she traveled. As she climbed the bank of the river to find shelter for a much-needed rest she stopped abruptly and froze in her tracks. Her keen nose had detected wood smoke made by burning pine knots. Burning pine knots at this time of year could only mean one thing-they came from a campfire. Could it be that Grey Eagle's men had outdistanced her and were waiting on the trail ahead? Impossible, thought Metonka. Someone else must be in the area-but who could it be?

Metonka reasoned that whoever had built the early morning campfire could certainly not be aware of her presence. She had approached the area in darkness. If it was not Grey Eagle's campfire then whoever had built it would not be expecting her. At the moment it was still too dark to survey the dense forest in an attempt to find the exact location of the fire, so Metonka sought the cover of her favorite outdoor shelter, another large Norway spruce, and hid from potential prying eyes. Snug in her temporary refuge, she realized that her tracks were now completely visible along the river, leading directly to her present hiding place. Too fatigued to erase the tell-tale tracks and too confused to untangle the new mystery before her, Metonka fell asleep, content with the realization that she would deal with the owner of the fire when she awakened.

At that moment, on the bank of the Skeena River about a half mile from the place where Metonka had sought refuge under the Norway Spruce, Barney finished his cup of tea and began to bank the fire, knowing that Louie would be there within the next eight hours. Barney was now two-thirds of his way around the trapline circuit, and only a day's journey from the cabin. The clockwise route that the trappers had chosen, with Barney one day ahead of Louie, had worked to perfection until recently when Louie had begun extending the route in search of beaver along the river.

As Barney stowed his pelts and cooking utensils on the sled he was unaware that a stranger had entered the territory that the trappers had assumed was their private domain. As he adjusted the shoulder harness of the sled, which he used now that cold weather allowed him to easily move its runners across the snow-covered surface, he relished the thought of spending a night in the warm cabin. Most of all, the stove and utensils in the cabin would allow him to cook the venison steaks that he had stored in the cache.

His mouth watered as he thought about the meal of steaks, canned green beans, powdered mashed potatoes, and hot bannock, which he intended to make from the generous supply of flour that remained. He also suffered a pang of conscience for Louie because there was no evidence that Louie ever cooked anything beyond opening containers of meat and vegetables, often heating them in their original cans by immersing them in boiling water. On days when Barney occupied the cabin he made a habit of leaving portions of roasts, steaks, and bread for Louie because he realized that Louie would not cook such foods for himself. He knew that his efforts were appreciated because there were never any leftovers when Barney returned to the cabin two days later.

As Barney anticipated completing the circuit that would by late afternoon take him to the trappers' cabin, Louie, a day farther to the north, kicked aside the double folds of his Hudson's Bay blanket and searched for the boots that on the previous evening he had set between his lean-to and the fire. Next he warmed his hands over the fire that was now a smoldering bed of coals. Additional twigs soon produced the kind of blaze that he needed to cook his breakfast. Powdered eggs and strips of venison jerky fried in bacon grease constituted his morning meal, topped off with a pot of hot water for his favorite beverage, green tea.

Louie had no complaints about the life he was leading—complaining was not part of his personality, but he was getting a bit tired of the routine that more and more found him talking to himself as he moved along the trapline. This morning as he waited for the fire to sufficiently heat the frying pan, his mind wondered to a restaurant, any restaurant where he could order a thick steak, complete with a baked potato, and a large piece of apple pie. He was glad that this phase of the homesteaders' duties was almost over.

Another two trips around the trapline and they would be heading to Prince Rupert with what both trappers considered to be a bonanza in prime furs. Refreshed by the thoughts of great food and a more leisurely lifestyle, Louie completed the preparation of his simple meal and resumed his journey, inspecting the traps along the streams that flowed into the Skeena River.

Metonka awoke from her nap, realizing that her exhausting journey had caused her to sleep longer than she intended. By the height of the sun she guessed that it must be near noon. Her keen sense of smell still detected wood smoke, but now the smell seemed to permeate the entire area. She could not tell its source, but she knew that she was ravenously hungry. She associated campfires with food, and her empty stomach told her that perhaps someone had left scraps of food around the campfire. She knew that if she was to resume her previous pace she would have to find food soon. The small supply of jerky that she had hidden in her pack without arousing the suspicion of Grey Eagle's wives had been devoured yesterday, so now the need for food dominated her thinking.

As she parted the overhanging branches of the Norway spruce tree, preparing to step into the little clearing that overlooked the valley, she caught a flash of something reflected in the bright sunlight. The flash had been a long distance away, nearly across the valley, but the brightness could not be mistaken. Instinctively, she knew that such a bright gleam did not exist in nature. The beam of light had been reflected from a man-made object such as mirror or a gun. Her sixth sense of survival told her the flash meant that men were in the area.

Hurriedly, she withdrew to the cover of the tree trunk and contemplated her next move. Did the flash come from weapons carried by Grey Eagle's men? The direction of the flash, north of her present location, suggested that it could have been made by Grey Eagle's men, but why would they be so far east of the river? If they were following her they should simply have followed the river as she had done. Nor would any attempt to intercept her have sent her pursuers so far off to the east. Were there other men, hunters perhaps, in the area? Metonka decided that she would move to the edge of the meadow, keeping her silhouette hidden by creeping low among the cedars, and attempt to find what or who had created the gleam of light.

Near the middle of the valley that contained the two homesteads Louie was busy removing a large beaver from a trap that Barney had set the previous day. With his .22 caliber pistol he dispatched the beaver, and reset the trap as Barney had taught him. After depositing the beaver on his sled he continued his journey along the stream. Unknown to him, it was the silver metal on his pistol that cast the gleam of light that alerted Metonka to his presence.

Although Louie was still nearly a mile away, Metonka's keen eyes could now see that the gleam was associated with a large figure, much larger than any of Grey Eagle's men. With a sigh of relief she realized that at least for the moment her pursuers were not visibly on her trail. With her greatest fear temporarily solved, she contemplated her next move. Should she approach the figure and ask for help? What if her request was refused? What if the man was an evil person who resented her presence? If she stayed out of sight and followed the man, would he lead her to food and shelter? By now her hunger had become so great that it was beginning to influence her decisions.

As Metonka pondered her next move she was astonished to see that the man seemed to be following a trail that would take him directly to the little clump of cedars in which she was hiding. From her vantage point overlooking the valley she could clearly see the man as he made his way along the stream. She saw him stop frequently stoop down and attend to something on the ground and then continue his journey. He did not seem to be in any hurry, but his deliberate walk told Metonka that he knew precisely where he was going. Her experience with trapping also told Metonka that the man was tending a series of traps, and that his final destination seemed to be the river near where she was hiding.

Metonka could not risk having the man discover her in the grove of cedars so she slipped her feet into her snowshoes and moved hurriedly in a southerly direction along the river. There was no time now to completely hide her tracks, so she cut a large bough from a cedar tree and swept it across her trail as she walked backward among the dense grove of young cedars. She realized that this evasive action would not deceive an experienced woodsman, but she hoped that the trapper would not come directly upon her tracks that day.

Drifting snow during the night would completely hide her tracks. Metonka had not anticipated being discovered at this point in her flight, but now there was nothing she could do but wait for the trapper to move past her. The pain in her stomach told her that she would soon have to find something to eat, but even if she snared a rabbit or partridge, starting a fire to cook it was out of the question. She may have to resort to stealing the meat and fish that the trapper was using for bait and eat raw whatever she found if she could not quickly satisfy the gnawing feeling in her stomach.

Louie completed his inspection of the traps that constituted the second phase of the trappers' circuit and began his climb out of the valley to the little rise that led to his evening's shelter. It was two o'clock, with plenty of time to skin the beaver and two mink that made up his catch for the day. As he moved toward the higher ground he had the uncanny feeling that he was being watched. Knowing that the only other human being, Barney, was a full day ahead of him and by now probably in the cabin, Louie dismissed the thought and shuffled his snowshoe-clad feet toward his evening camping spot. Try as he might to entertain other thoughts, he could not shake the feeling that eyes were peering from somewhere, watching his every move. As he schussed over the drifted snow he reflected on the eerie silence of the wolves during the last several evenings. What was causing them to change their musical communication?

As Louie entered the grove of cedars he came to an abrupt stop. There, as plain as could be, was the imprint of a snowshoe. A careful examination of the print told Louie that it was made by someone other that Barney because the snowshoe that made the print was wider and shorter than those worn by either Barney or he. Mountie Mackenzie had told Barney and he to buy snowshoes with an extended, rather than a rounded point in order to keep the snowshoe from sinking into the snow as the wearer's weight moved forward. He scolded himself for not paying closer attention when Scott Mackenzie had shown them the various styles of snowshoes worn by the different Indian tribes, but at that time he had dismissed such information as having little consequence for him.

Despite Louie's lack of fear in almost any predicament, this unexpected situation caused the hair on his neck to bristle with anticipation. Who had made the track? Louie could tell that the print was less than an hour old because it had been made while the crusted snow was melted. No snow had drifted into the print, giving further evidence that the track was fresh. Louie realized that whoever had made the track was most likely watching him that very moment. This unexpected finding had placed him in a mild state of alarm, so he tried to calm himself, knowing that he would have to think clearly about his next action. Where was the intruder hiding? Was Louie in someone's gun sight at this moment?

Closer inspection of the snowshoe print told him that it had been made by a person much lighter that he or even Barney. From previous experience he was familiar with the depth of Barney's tracks. Even though this print was wider than the snowshoes Barney wore, the print was only one-half as deep. Why was there only one print? Further examination of the area soon revealed that the wearer had tried to hide the trail by brushing the snow behind him. If that was true then the intruder was not really behind Louie, as the print seemed to indicate, but was perhaps hiding in the trees to the south.

Having recovered his sense of calm, Louie's keen mind now burst into action. If the intruder was intent on killing him he could easily have done so while Louie approached the cedar grove, and before Louie was aware of his presence. The fact that the trespasser tried to hide his tracks was evidence that he did not want Louie to know he was in the area. But why would anyone try to hide? In the north country it was a custom to provide food and shelter to anyone and everyone, no questions asked. Perhaps the person was running from someone. Did he really come from the north? If he had traveled up the river from the south he would have come upon the cabin and most likely Barney would have seen him. As Louie pondered these questions he moved into a thick stand of young cedars so that his actions would not betray to the intruder that Louie had discovered his presence.

Louie then recalled that Scott Mackenzie had told them of Indian tribes to the far north that sometimes followed the migrating wood caribou south to the Skeena valley in the fall. Mackenzie further observed that it had been so long since anyone had heard from them that he was not sure they were still in the area. Some of the Indian tribes had gravitated to and sought shelter and assistance from the forts in the area and thereby lost interest in their former way of life.

Louie further recalled that the official at the Homesteads Claims Office had mentioned, in passing, that a group of the Inland Tlingit Indians regarded the entire area as belonging to them because the area was encompassed by their ancient hunting grounds. He, too, had no knowledge of any hunting or trapping activity by Indians in the area during recent years. Perhaps, reasoned Louie, the Indians had sent a scout ahead to report on the prospects of game. Perhaps it was a lone Indian who merely enjoyed the solitary life that such an excursion provided. Whatever the situation, Louie knew that he had to discover who had encroached on their homestead, and try to learn the intruder's intentions.

Louie reasoned that if the impending contest of dispatching the intruder depended on physical strength he would be more that a match for any man. Therefore, he planned to resume his trip to the campsite as naturally as possible. When he came to a good place for an ambush he would hide and wait to see if anyone was following him. If so, he would spring upon the man and wrestle him to the ground before any weapons could be entered into the fray. With this in mind, he set off through the cedar grove at a rapid pace. As soon as he came to a narrow passage between two clumps of trees he slipped off the trail and doubled back to a place where he could watch the trail and yet be well hidden.

Barely had he settled into his hiding place when he noticed a figure creeping along the trail he had just left. As the figure passed his hiding place Louie sprang out, wrapped his giant arms around the figure, and wrestled it to the ground. The figure let out a scream and reached into its waist, unsheathed a long-bladed hunting knife. Louie, anticipating such an act, grasped the wrist and twisted the opponent's arm until the knife dropped to the snow.

"My god, it's a girl!" exclaimed Louie when he thrust back the parka that covered his victim's head. "What you are doing way out here in the wilderness?"

"Get off," demanded the fur-clad prisoner. "Metonka running from her man. Can you help?"

"Well, that depends," responded the amiable Louie, now relieved that the incident had ended without any anticipated violence. "Why don't we go to my campsite, which is only a short distance from here and then you can tell me all about your troubles."

After retrieving Metonka's knife, which Louie placed in his knapsack, he set off to the campsite with Metonka close behind. Louie had detected that the Indian girl was harmless, but half-starved, so when they reached the campsite he produced from this knapsack the venison jerky and bannock that remained from his lunch. Metonka devoured these remnant scraps so rapidly that Louie wished he had not consumed such a large share of his provisions for the noon meal. Realizing that his new acquaintance was famished, he hooked eight fat rainbow trout out of the beaver pond. He placed the fish on his wooden grid, fanned the coals that remained from Barney's early morning fire and soon had a feast of broiled trout ready for his hungry guest.

Soon the two campers were enjoying a feast of fish that can be appreciated only by individuals who have been exposed to vigorous activity in the open air for long hours. A pan of bannock, fried in bacon grease completed the evening meal. When Louie had satisfied Metonka's hunger he sat opposite her on the logs that served as camp stools and asked her to tell her story.

As the blazing fire warmed the two campers, Metonka eagerly responded to Louie's incessant questions. Within the next hour Louie extracted from Metonka her complete history, including why she was fleeing her people and how she had eluded her pursuers. The conversation that transpired proved to be an excellent example of Louie's naiveté regarding perception and reality. Metonka's convincing account of her escape persuaded Louie that she had every right to leave her village and that she had, indeed, deceived Grey Eagle and his men into thinking that she had gone back to her grandmother's village.

If Louie had seen Metonka's panic-stricken actions earlier that day he may not have been so willing to accept the confident account that she now reconstructed of how she had outwitted her potential pursuers. However, Metonka correctly surmised that her only chance of joining Louie in his journey to Prince Rupert was dependent on his belief that her tribe had by now given her up for lost, and therefore, would not any longer seek her return.

As Metonka and Louie conversed into the evening hours Louie realized how much he had missed the sound of a human voice. Barney, he admitted, had been correct in surmising that Louie would greatly miss daily contact with other human beings. As

Metonka spoke in her soft, seductive voice, Louie was completely mesmerized by her story. The sight of the beautiful Indian girl, dressed in her buckskin skirt, with her long, black hair falling over her shoulders, completely disarmed Louie. So engrossed was he in her tale of hunger, hardship, and love sent awry that he failed to comprehend that he was once again a victim of his own illusions about fairness and injustice. He failed to consider that in Metonka's account he was receiving only one version of a complex story-one that involved a culture far different from his own and one which required a more unbiased judgment than he was able to render under the circumstances.

Even if Louie had initially entertained doubts about Metonka's version of her life story he was no longer in a mood to question her motives. Furthermore, the calculated method that she had chosen to obtain her freedom brought out a sense of admiration that Louie found difficult to hide. In fact, he was so impressed by Metonka's three-day, thirty-mile trek on snowshoes that he quickly dismissed any questions or doubts about the rest of her amazing story. Although he should have been greatly concerned about the potential danger involved if Metonka's people attempted to pursue her, he took no more than his usual precautions in securing his food, furs, and weapons prior to preparing his camp for the night. Metonka had convinced the gullible Louie that she had skillfully eluded her followers.

It was this state of admiration, almost to the point of reverence, that prompted Louie to invite Metonka to share his blanket that evening. The next morning he wrote on the slip of birch bark that he and Barney used as a message system the following terse note: *Found Indian girl on trail. Shared blanket with her. Slept warmer. She will come with me on trapline and then to P. Rupert. Louie.*

Louie knew that Barney would be furious when he saw the note, but he felt that once Metonka's plight was known to Barney he would understand and consent to have the Indian girl accompany them to Prince Rupert. Louie reasoned that as only four days of trapping remained, there was no way that reasonable men could send the Indian girl back to face her tribe, knowing what Metonka had told him about the harsh justice that awaited her from her husband and his other wives. Sending Metonka ahead to Prince Rupert without someone to assist her would also surely result in disaster, even if she was able to complete the two hundred and eighty mile journey along the Skenna River by herself. Satisfied that this reasoning would be sufficient to obtain Barney's grudging consent, Louie thrust the note into the message box and prepared to complete the final leg of the trapping circuit with Metonka as his companion.

As Louie and Metonka followed the trail along the river toward the trappers' cabin Louie's admiration for Metonka's stamina and skills grew by the hour. Twice she hurled her body into a deep snow drift, each time emerging with a ruffed grouse clutched in her bare hands, which she quickly dispatched by twisting off its head. When Louie asked, "How do you know where they are?" Metonka showed him the slight depressions in the snow bank, devoid of any other marks. "Bird flies into snow to keep warm," explained Metonka.

Louie also discovered that Metonka was adept at breaking a trail through the deep drifts, making it easier for him to pull the sled, loaded with yesterday's animals, which he had neglected to skin, plus those that they acquired along the way. When they paused for lunch Metonka quickly built a fire, despite Louie's apprehension about the visibility of the telltale smoke to potential prying eyes. Before Louie could complete his protest she had placed the plucked grouse on two poplar skewers and prepared to roast them over the fire. Before the hour had elapsed Louie experienced another milestone-a hot noon-day meal while on the trapline. Previously, his lunch had consisted of bannock and bacon leftover from breakfast.

Having completed the last leg of the trappers' circuit, Louie introduced Metonka to the trapper's cabin. Metonka was amazed and delighted to spend the night in such a spacious, heated structure. Metonka had little experience with iron stoves, but she soon learned the mechanics of feeding the fire through the hinged door. The controlled heat that emerged from the stove top, minus the smoke of the campfire, further demonstrated to her that the white man's way of life was superior to the one she had known.

Before Louie had finished skinning the beaver and three mink that constituted his two-day catch Metonka had prepared a feast of potatoes, green beans, and venison steak. As a bonus she had roasted the beaver's tail, which she had persuaded Louie to separate from the carcass before he began to remove its skin. Once again Louie was overwhelmed with the results of the meal that Metonka set before him. Part of the gratitude stemmed from his own inadequacies as a cook, but even the most finicky gourmet, after having participated in that evening's meal, would have agreed that Metonka's culinary skills were outstanding.

In the short time Louie had known Metonka she had fulfilled three of his most basic needs. Although Metonka did not realize at the moment how greatly she had ingratiated herself to Louie, she could tell that Louie was surprised and pleased with her abilities. Louie, in the meantime, had resolved that there was no way anyone could convince him to send Metonka back to her people. If Barney insisted on traveling to Prince Rupert without Metonka, Louie would take his share of the furs and travel with Metonka. Louie had determined that Metonka would remain with him at least until they were safely in Prince Rupert.

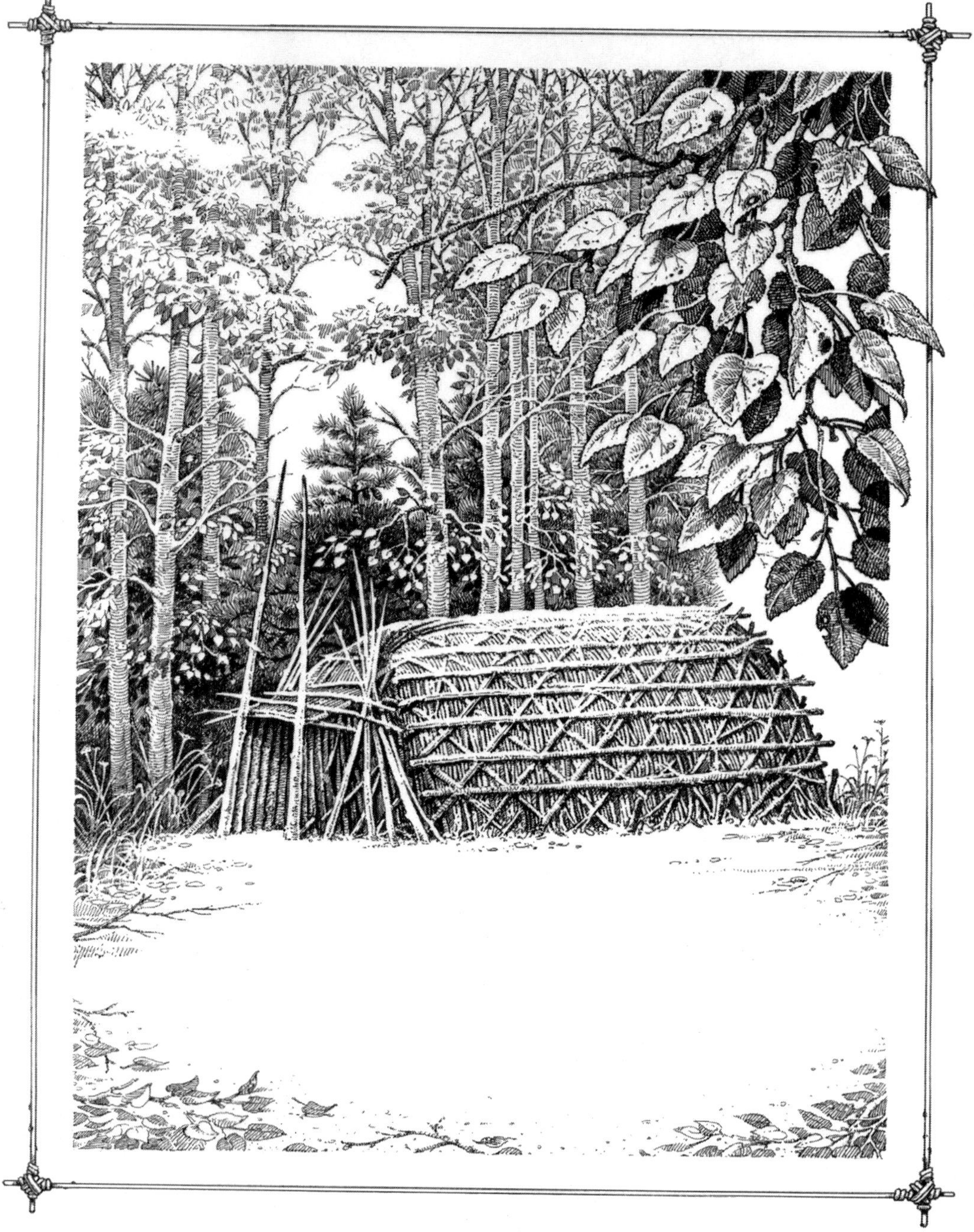

Chapter 11

Visitors in the Valley

Barney, having completed his inspection of the traps between the first and second outposts of the trapline, left the trail and moved to a knoll that overlooked the entire valley. This vantage point had become a favorite place for him to spend a few minutes of relaxation before he entered the dark grove of conifers that served as the trappers' second outpost. Today, as he surveyed the country to the north, his keen eyesight detected what appeared to be a faint column of gray-black smoke rising vertically near the foothills of the Babine Mountains.

Startled by what he saw, Barney kept his eyes focused on the spot while he frantically searched his pack for his binoculars. Although the wisp of smoke had been quickly dispersed by the wind, Barney was certain that his eyes had not deceived him. His present vantage point did not allow him to view the valley floor from which the smoke must have come. Smoke to the north meant trouble. Barney knew that Louie should be one day behind him on the trapline, so the smoke could not possibly be from Louie's campfire, even if he had wandered off course, as had been his habit lately. Besides, if Louie had left the trapline in one of his exploratory ventures why would he be building a fire this early in the afternoon? Barney knew that whoever had built the fire was not scheduled to be in the area, according to the authorities in Prince Rupert.

With fully two hours before sunset at his discretion Barney was determined to learn who had so boldly and conspicuously moved into the territory north of their homesteads that Scott Mackenzie had told them was "crown land." Hurriedly, he stored his sled beneath a large juniper that stood near the trail, placed the strap from his binoculars around his neck, and shouldered his .30 Remington. As he strode swiftly toward the high ground on the east side of their homesteads he thought of the possibilities that could account for the smoke. None of the possibilities relieved his anxiety.

During the last several days he had been convinced that the rhythm of life throughout the entire valley had been changing. The resident wolf pack, with its predictable calls for the evening hunt, had been unusually quiet. Greater numbers of caribou and deer had come to the valley from hills in the north during the last three days, although it was too early for them to begin herding up for the winter. Was something or someone disrupting the animals' routine? Barney did not know, but he intended to learn if there was some association between the smoke and what he perceived as a disrupted balance of nature in the valley.

After traveling north for four miles along the high country Barney came to a knoll that extended for several hundred yards. There he located a hemlock tree that reached upward nearly eighty feet. By climbing to its top Barney would have a commanding view of the entire country to the north. Slipping out of his snowshoes, Barney shifted the hand ax that he carried in a sheath on his belt to

one side so that it would not interfere with his climbing, adjusted his rifle so it rode diagonally over his back and began to climb the monarch hemlock tree. During the several minutes it took him to climb the tree he was forced several times to unsheathe his ax in order to cut away obstructing branches. Barney soon found himself positioned near the top of the hemlock, nearly seventy feet above the ground.

The sight that greeted Barney as he swung his 12 × 40 binoculars across the valley caused him to cling more tightly to the trunk of the swaying tree. There, less than four miles away, in a meadow along the edge of the river stood three Indian lodges. Mountie Mackenzie had told Barney that, typically, each lodge would house an entire family, but in a hunting party a lodge would most likely be inhabited by four or five men. As Barney trained his glasses on the lodges he could see figures moving about. From their actions, which involved activities around a large, centrally located fire, Barney surmised that the four or five persons in the encampment were women. After watching for approximately fifteen minutes he also detected the presence of several dogs, but no additional figures made their appearance. If this was a deer hunting party the men would be out until dark-the most productive part of the hunting day.

The presence of an Indian hunting camp so close to the homesteaders' land presented a problem to Barney. He recalled that the factor at the Office of Land Management had told them that the subarctic culture of Inland Tlingit and Tutchone Indians regarded the land assigned to Barney and Louie as theirs, but the factor had dismissed these claims of ownership as inconsequential and suggested that it was nothing about which the homesteaders should be concerned.

"All this land is Crown land," proclaimed the factor. "Legally, it is ours to distribute as homesteads on a first-come, first-served basis. If the native people want to occupy the land, they will have to file for it just as you are. We have reports from trappers that there are bands of nomadic Indians, but we don't even know how many there are or where they are. We have no reports of any trappers or prospectors seeing Indians in that country for the past ten years."

Barney realized that the Indians' encampment was some distance from their homesteads, but if the Indians laid claim to all the land in the valley they would surely feel that Barney and Louie were trespassing. Barney was not so sure the issue of land ownership would be as easily dismissed by the Indians as the factor had presumed.

As Barney surveyed the situation it occurred to him that perhaps the Indians had not detected the homesteaders' presence. With only four days left in their planned trapping season, Barney reasoned that if he and Louie concealed their movements, they would be able to move out of the country before the Indians detected them. If possession of lands became a problem Barney was content to let the Bureau of Indian Affairs in Prince Rupert deal with the issue next spring. At the moment all Barney wanted was for Louie and he to safely exit the area with their bonanza of furs.

As Barney climbed down from his lofty perch he considered several options. Every phase of the trapping venture had gone so well that he wanted to avoid any problems during these last several days. Should he reverse his route, intercept Louie, and tell him what he had discovered? Should he begin picking up the traps from the second and third phases of the circuit and then intercept

Louie while Louie journeyed along the first part of the circuit? After mulling over the alternatives, Barney decided that he would collect the traps as he completed the second and third portions of the circuit, deposit the traps and furs at the cabin site and then intercept Louie two days hence as he started toward their first outpost. In this way he and Louie could retrieve the traps along the first phase of the circuit and conclude the year by traveling counterclockwise to the cabin.

Satisfied that he had made the correct decision, Barney returned to his campsite for what he considered to be his next to last evening of skinning animals and cooking meals by the light of a campfire. Sleeping under a lean-to shelter with the howling wolves as his only evening companions had also become wearying. Although Barney still relished the freedom of the wilderness, three months of living in an uncompromising environment, especially in the bitter cold and snow of November, had convinced him that hot meals, clean clothes, and a kapok mattress with a roof over it would be a welcome change.

After coaxing the lighted birch bark and cedar twigs to ignite the dry logs that he had selected for his camp fire Barney prepared what he presumed to be one of his last meals in the open air of the Canadian wilderness. He reflected on the successful season that their homesteads and this beautiful country had provided as he skinned the day's catch of three mink and two pine marten. However, that night he slept fitfully. The unexpected presence of other human beings whose intentions he did not know somehow seemed ominous beyond explanation. He chastised himself for attributing so much importance to the presence of unidentified campers to the north, but try as he would he was unable to dismiss his apprehensions. Sleep, the elixir of tired woodsman, eluded him as he tossed restlessly upon the spruce boughs that had on previous evenings provided such a welcome break from the physical demands of the trapline.

"It's Thanksgiving Day," Barney announced the next morning, mostly in surprise to himself as he checked his pocket calendar. Despite spending a restless night in his lean-to, this morning there was a spring in his gait as he set off on snowshoes to retrieve the traps from the second phase of the circuit. As the sun peeked over the eastern slope of the Babine Mountains he pulled his watch from his side pocket and discovered that it was nearly eight o'clock. The sun's steady departure to the south of the equator had shortened the hours of daylight considerably, making it difficult for the trappers to complete their portion of the circuit during the eight hours now available to them.

"Time to head back to civilization," Barney mused, as he considered the increased difficulty that the shortened hours of daylight posed for human beings in the wilderness. The animals, too, seemed to be less active as the daylight waned. When hunger drove them from of their nests and dens they were prone to hunt along the trails, making the trappers' bait all the more effective, but also tempting as a food supply to the larger predators. This morning as he trudged through the newly drifted snow Barney's thoughts frequently turned from his trapline to family and friends a long way from British Columbia. Although harvesting furs continued to be productive, this morning he was content to call it a season-a very productive season-and retreat to the comforts of civilization.

"I wonder what Louie will tell me today?" questioned Barney as he pulled the last trap from its cubby and placed it on the sled along with nineteen others, ready to be placed in the fur cache until next year. Next he placed the unused bait in the fork of a tree so that some fortunate creature, bird or animal, might have a Thanksgiving Day feast. As he approached the message box a smile came to his face. He recalled the numerous written messages that he and Louie had exchanged during their eighty-five days on the trapline.

Notes that Barney left in the message boxes were brusque and forthright, reflecting his lack of facility with the English language. Louie's notes, on the other hand, seemed always to fill the entire birch bark sheets. He wrote jokes and rhymes, and when there was nothing important to report he filled the sheets with bits of songs that seemed to be going through his active mind. However, the message that Barney received today, written in Louie's legible style, caused Barney to curse aloud.

"Damn it, Louie," muttered Barney as he reread Louie's note. Suddenly the smoke and the Indian village that he had seen yesterday all seemed to fit into a complex picture that now involved Barney and Louie. Barney had been told by the bartender in Prince Rupert, in a teasing manner, that it was common for Indian girls to run away from their villages to live with the white trappers. He also pointed out the consequences of such actions. Most often the white trappers tired of the Indian girls' companionship when they returned to civilization. Such actions left the Indian girls without any alternative but to return to their own people. Scott Mackenzie frowned on such unions and saw them as merely acts of convenience on the part of the white trappers.

Louie's note intensified the feeling of apprehension that had plagued Barney the last several days, but which until now he had been unable to identify. Suddenly the strategic plan to end the trapping season and the timely exit to Prince Rupert seemed in jeopardy.

"Indian woman is trouble. Send her back!" wrote Barney, angrily shoving the note into the message box. As he reconsidered his note, he realized that his terse warning was not likely to influence Louie. Besides, it would be late tomorrow before Louie would read the note, having reached this leg of the circuit.

The new information that confronted Barney told him that he would have to abandon his plan to continue clockwise throughout the entire circuit. He decided that he would first deposit his traps and furs in the cabin and then reverse his direction, thereby intercepting Louie at a point along the trapline farthest from their cabin, but nearest the Indian village. Even though it was a day's journey from the farthest point of the trapline to the Indian encampment, Barney reasoned that confronting Louie and the Indian woman at that location presented the best hope of persuading her to return to her people.

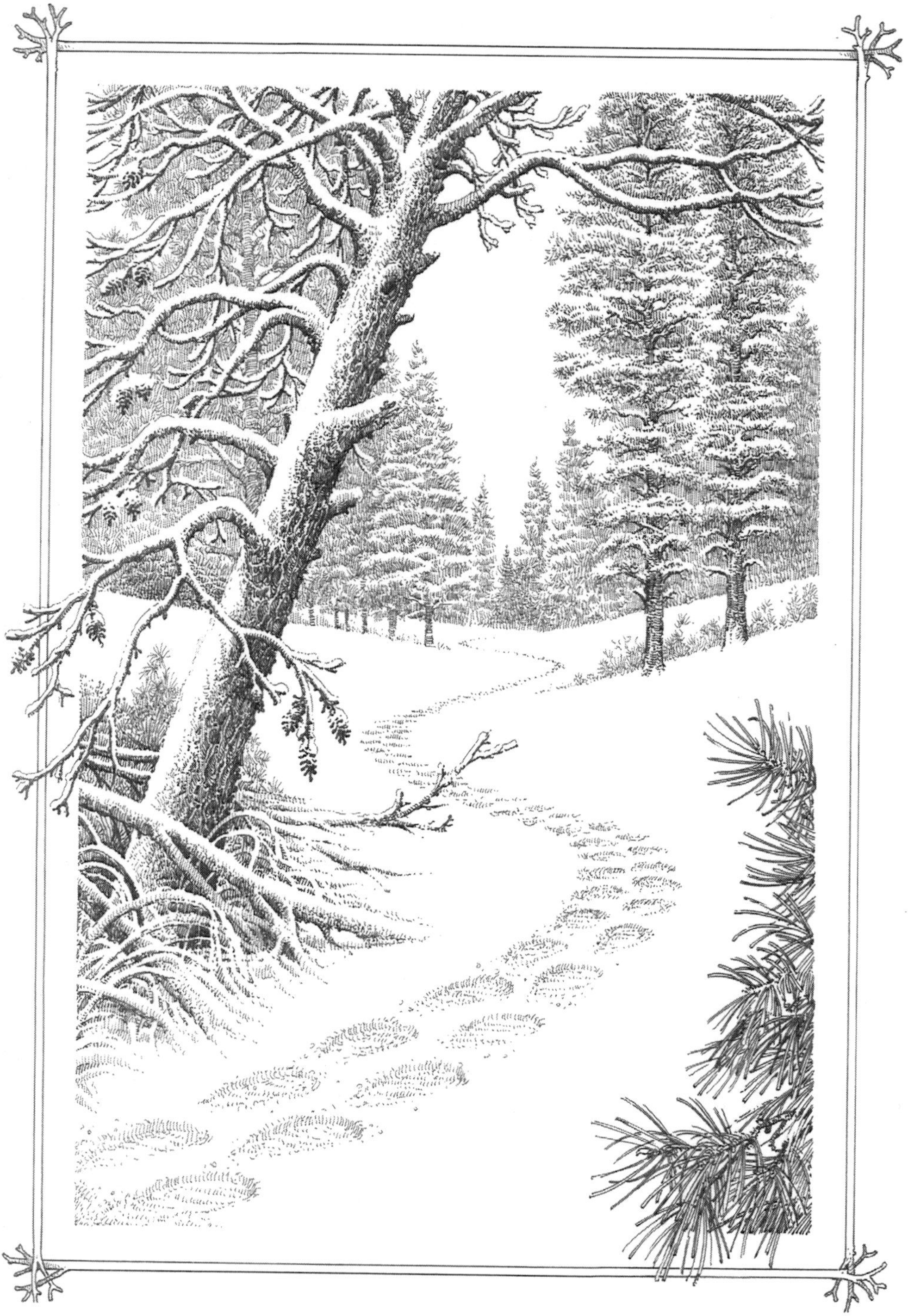

Chapter 12

Louie Is Missing

Once Barney had reaffirmed his plan to intercept and rescue Louie from his venture into amorous irrationality he retrieved the remaining traps along the third phase of the circuit and headed for the cabin. There he stored the furs and traps in the cache. Despite his concern for the predicament in which Louie had placed them, he allowed himself a moment to marvel at the success of the trapping venture. As he deposited the furs he could not help but relish the success of the season, reflected in the row upon row of pelts which hung by strings tied to the poles suspended from the gable ends of the building. Assessing quickly, he counted forty-eight beaver, forty mink, eighteen otters, four fishers, twelve marten, and fifteen foxes. Missing was the silver fox about which Louie had fantasized earlier. The early frost and the continuing cold weather had produced prime fur conditions-a result that he hoped would not be lost to the fur traders in Prince Rupert.

Barney's delight at the sight of a small fortune in furs was short-lived. He knew that there were more pressing responsibilities at the moment. After a hearty meal of moose steak and potatoes he stored his nonexpendable supplies in the cabin and then prepared for an early morning departure to meet Louie and his Indian companion. Barney was determined that he would be able to persuade Louie that taking the Indian girl to Prince Rupert with them was pure folly. Louie had been impractical at times, but he had always listened to reason. Barney presumed that logic on this occasion would produce similar results.

Early the next morning Barney packed a two-day's supply of food, folded his Hudson Bay blanket and placed them in his knapsack. As he considered his mission he placed a second box of ammunition for his .30 Remington into the pocket of his Mackinaw jacket, hoping that he would not have to use it. He debated momentarily about taking his sled, but decided against it. Louie would have his sled, with sufficient food and cooking utensils for the one night that Barney expected them to sleep outdoors under the lean-to. Any animals that had been caught would have been skinned by the time Barney reached Louie; hence, there was no need for a second sled. Walking on snowshoes without having to pull a sled would also allow Barney to move twice as fast over the crusted snow.

A gentle falling snow greeted Barney the next morning as he opened the cabin door for his trek across the meadow where he hoped to intercept Louie. However, the air lacked its usual chilling effect, signifying to Barney that this might be the start of what Mountie Mackenzie had termed "the big snow." With a modified hop-running stride that he calculated would allow him to reach Louie by mid-afternoon, Barney set out on a mission that he was convinced could have only one outcome. Louie's Indian companion would have to return to her village. There was no alternative. To Barney's way of thinking, any repercussions that resulted from the Indian girl being sent home were neither his nor Louie's problem.

As he journeyed along the high ground on the east side of their homestead he deliberately determined not to spend anymore time worrying about a matter which he intended to resolve as soon as he met Louie. Instead, his thoughts turned to the beauty of the new fallen snow on the spruce and hemlock trees. He marveled once again at the beautiful country that had been granted to them as part of the Canadian Dominion Lands Act. For someone who loved unadulterated woods, streams, and meadows this was a perfect setting. Barney wondered if civilization would ever find its way to this valley and erode its tranquility by bringing in the sights and sounds of motorized vehicles.

Several hours of steady travel over the crusted snow, now covered with three inches of new snow, brought Barney to the trail on which Louie would be approaching from the north. Barney hoped that Louie had started out early that morning because the snow was now falling so heavily that only traces of yesterday's tracks remained. Dark storm clouds appeared in the west, indicating that a major storm was on the way. If Louie had begun his route early they would be able to meet soon. Depending on the time and condition of the storm, perhaps the men could travel cross-country and reach the cabin by evening, thereby eliminating the need to trudge through deep snow the following day.

After a brief rest Barney resumed his journey, noting that the swirling snow had completed obscured any trace of the trail that his snowshoes had made just a half hour earlier. Barney found himself locating trees for landmarks as he attempted to stay on the trail where he expected to find Louie. He knew that in this blinding snow Louie would do likewise. The swirling snow had intensified and wind gusts swayed the tops of the hemlock trees that lined the path where Barney intended to find Louie. Attempting to stray far from familiar territory in such weather would be folly, even for experienced woodsmen who were familiar with the country. Barney hoped that today Louie would exercise caution instead of resorting to his frequent spontaneous manner of making decisions without considering all feasible alternatives, a characteristic fault shared by both men, but one he failed to recognize in himself.

By noon Barney had covered two-thirds of his intended route. Why had Louie not made an appearance? What could cause him to be so late? Louie should have met him an hour ago. Was it possible that they missed each other in the blinding snow? Perhaps Louie had decided to stay in camp under the lean-to, thinking that the snow would stop, and at that time he could still complete the third part of the circuit. After all, Louie did not know that Barney had decided to intercept him by reversing the circuit and thereby come north to meet him along the way.

Barney's bewilderment over his failure to locate Louie turned his thoughts to the Indian girl. Perhaps Louie felt that traveling in the snow would be too difficult for her, and therefore had decided to wait another day before starting out. Perhaps the Indian girl knew that the storm would be severe and had persuaded Louie to delay his travels. These thoughts churned in Barney's mind as he grew ever more frustrated with the day's events. By mid-afternoon a foot of snow had fallen. The ever-present dark clouds suggested that the snowstorm would not end anytime soon. Barney realized that even if Louie and he met at this time it would be foolhardy to try to reach the cabin that evening. They would have to spend the night in the lean-to at the second outpost.

Barney acknowledged the awkwardness of having the Indian girl in their presence at a time when he was determined to send her away. But even in his anger, Barney could not consider driving her away without food and the assurance of a safe return to her village. He would cross that bridge when he came to it. The first priority now was to locate Louie. Then they would secure a warm, dry shelter for themselves and wait out the storm. As he pushed along the trail toward the lean-to Barney realized that anyone unfamiliar with the country could become hopelessly lost. He hoped that Louie had replenished the supply of firewood at the outpost because hunting for sufficient fuel to keep the fire going on such a night would be difficult. The lean-to would provide sufficient cover for the three of them this evening. A fire and a hot meal would provide the tranquil atmosphere that Barney needed to persuade Louie that his companion had no place in their plans for the future.

Shuffling through the deep snow delayed Barney's arrival at the lean-to campsite until late afternoon. Storm clouds and drifting wind intensified the gloom that encompassed the small clearing where the trappers had spent so many nights under the protection of the giant fur trees. To his dismay, Barney was not greeted by a roaring fire and the presence of Louie and his Indian companion. Inspection of the lean-to and the pile of wood told him that Louie had not visited the site. The message box, always a favorite place for Louie to contact Barney, still contained the note he had left the previous day. In fact, everything at the site was just as Barney had left it yesterday. Even the fire pit, with its usual banked pile of ashes over hot coals was now covered by a foot of snow.

Where was Louie? Even if he had delayed his travel for a day he should have reached this point along the circuit by now. Barney realized that the present site was also the point nearest the Indian encampment, but he was certain that Louie would not abdicate everything for which he had worked just for an excursion to the Indian village. He desperately felt the need to talk to Louie, aware that conversation had resolved their differences in the past. Barney wondered if Louie was so desperate for companionship that he would allow an Indian girl to persuade him to come to her village.

Barney decided that he could do nothing further that evening. He would build a fire, heat some food, dry his soaked outer garment, and sleep safely and dry in the lean-to. Tomorrow morning he would scout around the area to see if Louie had left any sign of his intentions. Perhaps Louie had encountered some difficulty on the first circuit of the trapline and headed back to the cabin. Perhaps he had anticipated the difficulty of traveling after the storm and headed cross-country to the cabin the previous day. In either case, Barney's search of the entire trapline would serve as a precautionary measure. If Louie was safe and snug in the cabin then the first major problem facing Barney at the moment would be solved. For a fleeting moment Barney considered the possibility that Louie was truly missing, but he refused to dwell on that thought. His life of self-sufficiency had taught him not to borrow trouble, but only to meet challenges when they could not be avoided. Barney refused to consider what his options would be if Louie was not in the cabin.

Barney awoke long before the first rays of the morning sun lighted the clearing adjacent to the campsite where he had spent the night. The storm had passed, but everything was covered with a deep blanket of powdery snow. On many other occasions Barney had paused to appreciate the beauty of the low-hanging branches with their snowy burdens, but this morning he was preoccupied with the thought of finding Louie. He realized the futility of looking for some sign of Louie in the snow, but if misfortune had befallen Louie there was a good possibility that he would have been able to find or build a shelter and survive for a time even without food or fire. With this in mind Barney packed his knapsack, slipped into his snowshoes, and scouted the numerous small groves of spruce and cedar trees that bordered their trapline.

By noon Barney was convinced that Louie and his Indian companion were not anywhere in the far corner of the first circuit, nor in the first portion of the second circuit of their trapline. He had already covered all of the remainder of the second and third portions of the trapline the previous day. The only remaining area to be searched was that part of the first circuit nearest the cabin. Barney knew that when he set out that afternoon he would have to reach the cabin by nightfall or risk a miserable night in the meadow without adequate shelter. However, the meadow would be easy to search because objects near the trail would be easily detected, even with the new covering of snow. Despite the ravages of the snowstorm Barney was convinced that Louie's ability as a woodsman would have been more than a match for whatever challenges nature threw at him. As he moved along his route he became acutely aware that the only chance of finding Louie safe and well depended on Louie having reached the cabin the previous day.

Trepidation overcame Barney as he approached the bend in the river which would give him the first sight of the cabin. What if Louie was not there? Louie had to be there. Barney had exhausted every means of finding him along the trapline. There were only two places where he could safely be-in their cabin or with the Indians at their encampment. Barney could not conceive of Louie having gone willingly to the Indians' encampment, but what was he to think if Louie was not at the cabin?

As the cabin came into view Barney's fear became reality. There was no telltale smoke rising from the chimney, which on such a clear day would have been visible for as far as the eye could see. One hope remained-Louie and the Indian girl may have taken Louie's share of the furs and departed for Prince Rupert, thereby avoiding Barney's opposition to having her accompany the trappers.

As Barney neared the cabin he realized that even such a possibility, implausible as it seemed, was far preferable to the alternative of having Louie disappear without a trace in the Canadian wilderness. He rationalized that if Louie was truly so enamored with the Indian girl that he would risk the wrath of his trapping partner by taking her to Prince Rupert without Barney, then Barney was prepared to understand the situation and forgive Louie's indiscretion, however incomprehensible such an action by Louie seemed at the moment. All the minor irritations the two trappers had endured during their three months in the wilderness would be forgotten if Louie was safe and healthy in Prince Rupert.

Barney opened the cabin door knowing that he would not find Louie there. Everything was as he has left it two days ago. There was no sign that Louie had been in the cabin. Inspection of the fur cache affirmed that all of the furs were just a Barney had left them. Somehow, Barney had known that Louie would not abandon him and their plans for the future under any conditions. Barney's momentary sense of relief was immediately swept away with the realization that now only three possibilities remained regarding Louie's whereabouts. Louie had either: gone willingly with his Indian companion to her village; been disposed of by the Indians or he was a captive in the Indians' settlement. Barney was convinced that Louie would not willingly join his Indian companion's people without some word of his intentions.

Barney had been unable to locate Louie's sled or any of his personal belongings, so he was convinced that Louie had been taken against his will. If Louie had gone to the encampment of his own free will he would have left some sign of his intentions. Even if Louie had been an unrestrained captive he would have left some sign that would allow an experienced tracker to follow his trail. The foot of new fallen snow had obliterated any signs that may have been left on the ground, but Barney's keen eye had not detected any broken branches or blazes among the trees along the trapline. Even though the two had never discussed the actions to be taken if such an emergency occurred, Barney was sure that had Louie been able to do so he would have provided some clues to serve as a guide for his partner.

Barney now assumed that Louie had been abducted without his consent. He did not know why the Indian girl had joined Louie, but the note indicated that he had courted trouble and somehow met with disaster. To Barney there was only one course of action. Tomorrow he would journey to the Indians' encampment and try to determine if Louie was in residence. In any event, Barney's goal was to reclaim his companion through whatever measures were necessary. If Louie was in the encampment Barney would find some way to persuade him that Prince Rupert was their logical winter destination.

With the thought of a rescue mission in mind, Barney loaded his sled with food, tarp, cooking utensils, and his trusted Hudson Bay blanket. If necessary, he was prepared to spend many days in the open, using his knowledge of the country to sustain him while he searched for his companion. Early the next morning, with his rifle slung over his shoulder, he placed his feet into his snowshoes and set off for what he anticipated to be a twenty-mile journey.

By mid-morning of his second day on the trail Barney reached the knoll from which he had initially seen the Indian's encampment. As before, he looped his binoculars around his neck and climbed the tall hemlock tree. Reaching the top, he secured his position and trained his binoculars on the snow-covered meadow. To his amazement the Indian lodges were no longer there. As he swept the valley and the adjacent hillsides he could find no trace of any living creature. The telltale smoke that had originally alerted him to the Indians' presence was nowhere to be seen. Clearly, the space that at one time had held the highly visible series of lodges was now a vacant place in the meadow. The Indians had left the valley without a trace, having moved before or during the snowstorm. This revelation caused Barney to grasp the trunk of the tree with both hands as his binoculars dropped to his chest, hanging from their tether. None of the scenarios that Barney had created during his journey to rescue Louie had included the prospect of not finding the Indian village in its previous location.

Barney slowly climbed down the huge hemlock tree, stunned by what he had just discovered. His plan of practical and feasible options for rescuing Louie was suddenly depleted. It would be reckless, daring, and dangerous to go into the Indians' country under any circumstances, and these were not ordinary circumstances. Barney had no clue about where the Indians were located, nor did he know how long ago they had vacated their encampment. If they had left before the snowstorm they would be two or three days beyond their former campground. No doubt they were aware of Barney's presence, because the Indian woman would surely have told them that Louie had a partner. With sufficient men to inhabit three lodges they could travel adequately and still set up guards along their back trail. Their dogs would also alert the Indians to anyone following them. Barney realized that the odds of finding and rescuing Louie under the present circumstances were strongly against the success of such an endeavor. Mountie Mackenzie's warning rang in his ears, "Be sure to come out by the first of December. If you are not out by then, no one will be able to reach you until late spring and the deep snow will prevent you from reaching Prince Rupert."

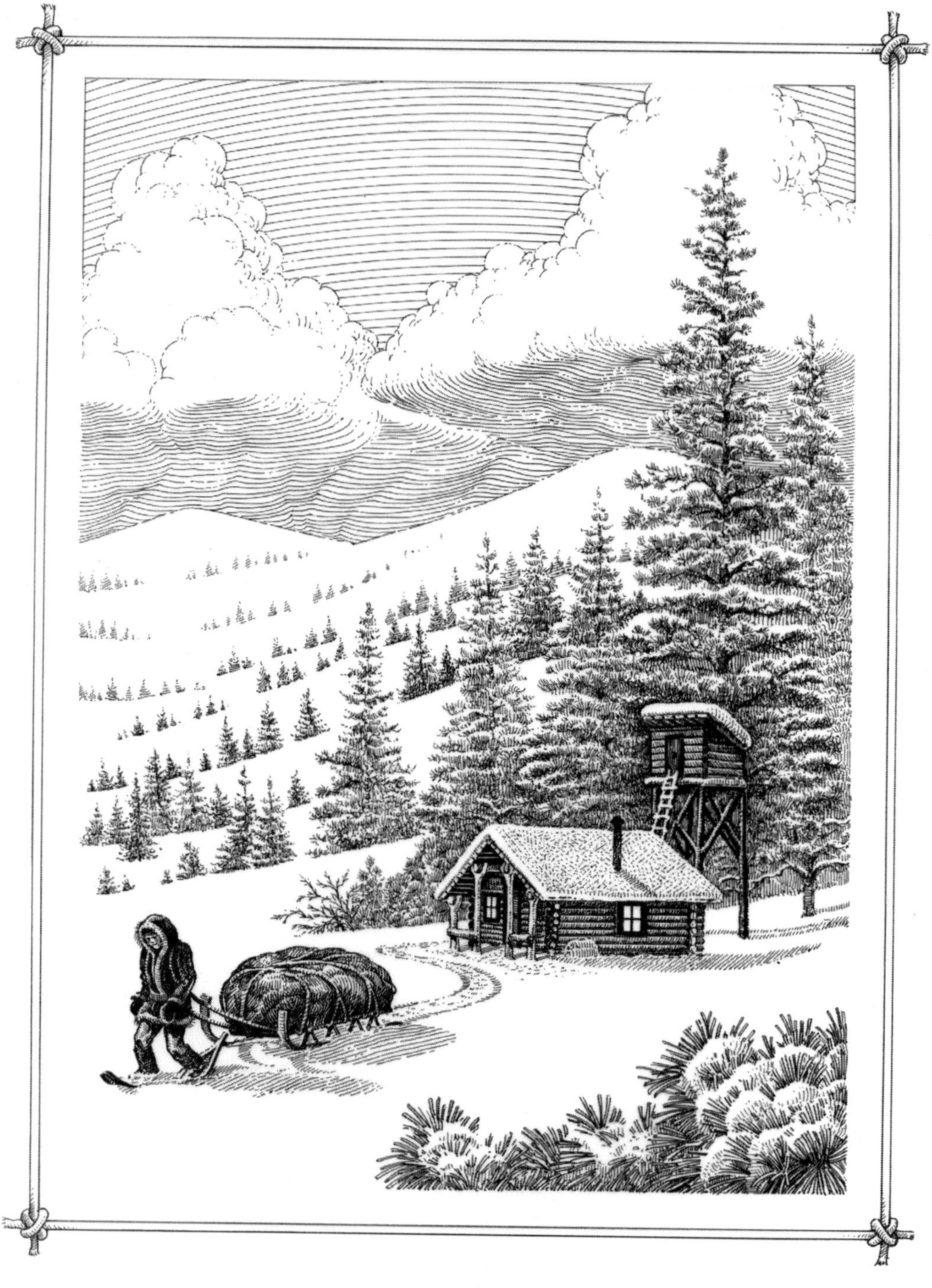

Chapter 13

Barney Leaves the Homestead without Louie

Barney sought the dry surface of a large rocky overhang from which he could see the entire valley to the north. The bright sunshine belied the gloom that had overcome him as he searched the Skeena Valley for any signs of life. As he recreated the events of the last four days it became clear that suddenly, and for the first time since he had been in the Canadian wilderness, the chain of events and his ability to regulate them were beyond his control. In prior emergencies there had always been a feasible action that, if executed properly, had produced a desirable outcome. The absence of the Indians' encampment eliminated such an option today.

With a heavy heart Barney retraced his steps to the cabin. He dreaded the thought of abdicating his efforts to locate Louie, but any attempt to continue the search under the present circumstances would surely end in disaster for both Louie and he. He was mindful of Scott Mackenzie's warning that the deep snows of December would prevent anyone from traveling in or out of the country. If he became trapped by the snow, without shelter, in an unfamiliar country, any chance of finding Louie would be lost.

Barney's calendar told him that tomorrow was December 1. Perhaps the snowstorms that Mackenzie had forecast were already underway. Mindful that becoming snowbound would erase any chance of finding Louie, he realized that the only logical choice remaining would make him look like a coward and a deserter. In Barney's code of living in the out-of-doors, one did not run away from friends who might need help.

By the time his journey brought him within sight of the cabin Barney had decided that only one option remained. Tomorrow he would load the furs on his sled and set out for the railroad construction site. The four-day journey would bring him in contact with a telephone line, through which he could contact authorities and report what he knew about his missing companion. With a sigh of contentment that he had considered all the possibilities and had settled on the only sensible course of action, Barney stored his sled under the canopy of the cabin, cooked his evening meal and prepared for the journey that awaited him the next morning.

Before retiring that evening Barney packed food, ammunition, and clothing for a week of camping along the Skeena River. Although there would be no ready-made shelters, to Barney the ability to provide a warm, dry refuge from the cold and snow did not pose a problem in this heavily wooded country. He would have to exercise care to prevent injury, which remained his only worry. He thought of how great it would have been with Louie by his side to share the joys and hardships of their successful exit.

Having completed his tasks within the cabin Barney retired to his bunk where he tossed fitfully about for several hours before abandoning the thought of sleeping. He set about rearranging the cabin, repacked the remaining food on shelves, and making a list of items that they would not need to purchase before returning next spring. By daylight Barney's sled was loaded with supplies and furs, ready for his trek to the railroad construction site.

Traveling along the Skeena River proved to be easier than Barney anticipated. The snow was now frozen into a crust that carried Barney's snowshoes over the hard surface, barely leaving an impression. A brisk northeast wind at his back seemed to energize the traveler and his sled as the miles vanished under his swift pace. Pausing only long enough to retrieve strips of jerky from the knapsack on his sled, Barney ate his meager fare as his snowshoes skimmed over the frozen river. By nightfall he had covered one-third of the distance to the construction site, nearly twice as far as he thought it possible to go in one day. If such ideal conditions continued he would be at the construction site by December 4.

A full moon illuminated the riverbed at 4:30 p.m. when Barney sought the shelter of a large windblown cedar tree as his campsite for the evening. He thumped the trunk repeatedly with his boots, causing the snow on the branches of the uprooted tree to drop in large clusters. Moving toward the middle of the tree, he chopped away the lower branches until a cave like opening took shape beneath the huge horizontal trunk. Using his snowshoes, he scooped away the snow that had fallen through the mass of branches, clearing the way for a mattress, which he made from cedar boughs. Soon a crackling fire warmed his evening meal and simultaneously dried his sweat-laden shirt and socks, which he had placed on a line out of reach from the sparks which shot skyward from the pitch in the cedar logs.

The temperature had fallen below zero degrees, but an abundant supply of wood assured Barney that he would have a comfortable night. The drifted snow formed a barrier around the lower branches of the tree, while the wind swept the heat of the fire into the lean-to. Twelve hours of pulling the sled full of supplies and furs had taken their toll on Barney's strength. Within minutes after wrapping himself between the layers of his Hudson Bay blanket he was asleep. For the first time in many nights he slept peacefully, confident that he had done all within his power to resolve the predicament in which Louie had placed them.

Morning found Barney rested and eager to resume his journey. He stowed his knapsack and cooking utensils on his sled, adjusted his shoulder harness, and set off for the riverbed. The sled of furs glided so smoothly behind him that at times he had to step aside as the sled skimmed past him, sliding down the elevations made by the drifted snow. How easily he traveled over the frozen ice in comparison to the trail-blazing efforts that Louie and he had endured in September as they cut a path through the brush and windfalls along the riverbank to reach their homesteads.

As he traveled westward Barney's mind returned repeatedly to the events of the last several days in an attempt to sort out what had gone so terribly wrong at a time when success and prosperity seemed to be within their grasp. Where was Louie today? Barney hoped that he was safe and warm in some Indian lodge-safe because Louie wanted to be there. The dreaded alternative was that Louie lay in an unmarked grave somewhere near the headwaters of the Skeena River, beyond the reach of white trappers, prospectors, and even the Canadian Mounted Police. Try as he might to remain optimistic about Louie's whereabouts, Barney had the premonition that Louie's disappearance was associated with a sinister outcome.

The third day of travel along the river found Barney in familiar country. He recognized the meadow where he had shot the six moose for the rail workers' food supply. As he rounded a small bend in the river he could see the shape of buildings looming ahead. To his surprise, the entire construction site seemed to be abandoned. Pulling his sled up the bank, Barney strode between the various sheds and bunkhouses. The new snow was devoid of tracks, indicating a lack of activity at the site for the last several days. Just when he was about ready to store his sled in one of the unoccupied sheds and use it for his evening's shelter he detected smoke coming from one of the small houses near the end of the housing units. His knock on the door was answered by a powerful voice, commanding, "Come in. It's open."

Barney pushed open the door and stepped into the blinding light of a gasoline lantern. Shielding his eyes from the glaring light he realized that he was staring into the twin barrels of a shotgun, aimed at his chest. "Who are you and what brings you out here at a time like this?" demanded the man behind the gun.

"I'm Barney Seefeldt, trapper on my way out to Prince Rupert," answered Barney.

"God, you look a sight," remarked the man behind the gun. "Come into the light, where I can see you."

As Barney complied he heard the gunman exclaim, "You're the moose hunter! I hardly recognized you with that beard and long hair." He lowered his shotgun and set it beside his chair, then he arose and assisted Barney in the removal of his snow-covered jacket and cap.

"Have you had supper?" questioned his host.

"Nope, haven't eaten since breakfast," offered Barney.

"Well, I'm about to cook supper. Why don't you join me? But first, let's get you into the washroom, where you'll find a scissors and razor so you can get rid of that hair. There's a mirror, so you can see what you're doing. Here's an extra lantern. I'll heat a pail of water so you can wash up." With that, the man showed Barney where he could make himself presentable.

After Barney emerged from the washroom his host extended his hand. "My name's Mike O'Neil. Call me Mike. The men refer to me as 'the straw boss' when they think I can't hear them?"

"Before I do anything else, can I use your telephone? I want to report my partner missing. I think he was kidnapped, and he may have been killed by Indians who came into our trapping territory just about a week ago." asked Barney.

"Line went dead with the last storm. Tree must have fallen over it somewhere. Nobody will try to fix it until next spring, so you'll have to wait until you get to Prince Rupert to file a report about your partner. Supper is ready, so sit down and eat, and when you're finished, you can tell me about you trapping experience and your missing buddy."

After a substantial meal of potatoes, carrots, and roast beef the two men settled in chairs before the big fireplace that warmed the cottage. As they sipped from cups of hot tea, Barney, not accustomed to long sessions of conversation, found himself responding to Mike's constant demands for more details about every phase of their wilderness adventures. Barney soon concluded that Mike was living vicariously through the experiences of the trappers, so he began to embellish his experiences with the details that Mike seemed to enjoy.

When Barney had finished describing his three months as a homesteader-trapper, Mike explained, "Your story made my hair stand on end just listening to it, much less living out there by yourself. What do you really think happened to Louie? After being alone all those months, don't you think it would have been easy for some Indian girl to talk him into going to her wigwam?"

"No, I don't," responded Barney. "Louie wasn't that kind of a person. He would not have gone off without telling me. Besides, he left a small fortune of furs behind. Louie knew how to spend money. With him it was 'easy come-easy go,' so I knew he was counting on the money to have a good time, and certainly not in an Indian village."

"Well, I don't think anyone will believe you when you tell them that you think your partner was kidnapped," replied Mike. "The Mounties have lived for years with filed reports that claimed trappers and prospectors were missing, only to have them turn up several years later, after having lived with Indian women, either in their own cabins or right in the Indian villages. Mounties get pretty tired of those routines, riding out in the cold and snow, trying to find someone, not knowing where to look, only to find out later on that the guy was snug and warm the entire time."

"Louie wasn't the kind of trapper or prospector that you described," protested Barney, but he could tell that Mike did not believe him. He wondered if his report would be received with similar skepticism when he filed it in Prince Rupert. After several pipes of tobacco the host stoked the fire once again. With conversation ebbing, the men agreed that it was time to seek the comfort of the bunks that lined the sides of the company-owned frame house.

Barney was grateful for the hospitality provided by Mike, but he was anxious to move on to Prince Rupert. Mike had invited him to stay until December 15, when Mike was to close the office. At that time the Canadian Pacific Railroad would send an engine out to retrieve Mike and any additional equipment that he needed for survival during his lone stay at the construction site. However,

Barney calculated that the journey on snowshoes to Prince Rupert along the rail line would take only four days, allowing him to reach his destination three days prior to Mike's arrival on December 15. After a hearty breakfast Barney bade Mike farewell, walked to the river, which he followed until he was able to climb onto the elevated rail tracks. With his snowshoes pointed westward between the two rails Barney leaned into the traces of his sled for the four-day journey that would take him to Prince Rupert.

The glow of Prince Rupert's street lights on the horizon became visible when Barney was still several miles from the city. The clear, cold air suggested that the city was deceivingly close, but Barney soon discovered that his impatient steps did not seem to cover the remaining distance nearly as fast as he anticipated. After nearly an additional hour of trudging along the tracks he reached the edge of Prince Rupert's main street. He remembered the hotel where he and Louie stayed in September, so he decided to seek food, shelter, and advice that evening and then tend to the remainder of his business on the following day.

The bright lights from the hotel's windows illuminated the snow-packed street as Barney pulled his sled up the steps leading to the porch that covered the entire front of the hotel. Although it was only five o'clock in the afternoon, the street was already dark and deserted except for a few dogs that were scavenging for food between the clapboard buildings. Barney was reluctant to leave the sled of furs for any length of time, so he hurriedly opened the door of the hotel. "Hello, stranger!" boomed a voice that Barney recognized as that of the clerk-bartender who had regaled them with stories during their stay in September.

"Hello," responded Barney. "Do you have room for me and a place to lock up my furs for the night?"

"Sure do," replied the clerk. "Room and three squares is one dollar a day. Bathroom with tub is next door. Two-bits for a bath. I'll store your furs in my garage without charge. I guess you'll want to sell them in town. How long do you plan to stay?"

"Sounds good to me," responded Barney, anxious to have the furs safely stored for the night. "I may stay two or three days, but I want to lock up the furs before I do anything else."

"I understand," announced the clerk. "Mary, will you tend the desk for a few minutes while I get this man's furs in our garage?" This pronouncement, which sounded more like a command than a request, prompted a middle-aged woman in a long-sleeved blouse and long skirt covered by a white apron to emerge from the kitchen where she apparently served as the cook, along with a host of other duties.

"Come on," motioned the clerk, grabbing a woolen cap and heavy jacket as he led the way out the door and down the snow-covered steps. "Gets pretty slow here after Thanksgiving Day. Everyone who is going somewhere has gone by now. What brings you out of the woods so late?"

"That's a long story," said Barney. "Lets get these furs stored, and then I'll tell you about it over a cup of coffee."

"Fair enough," suggested the clerk as they approached the garage attached to the hotel. Let's put your furs here. No one will bother them. Isn't anyone here to steal them, anyway. I'll lock them up and give you the key, if that makes you feel better."

"Good enough," responded Barney, happy to have control of the furs, but not entirely sure that the furs were safe in the rickety shed that served as the clerk's garage. "I'll get them out of here tomorrow morning and return the key to you then."

With the furs out of the way for the evening, Barney and the clerk make their way back to the hotel. "By the way, my name's Pat. Pat Shea," responded the clerk, offering his hand.

"Mine's Barney. You don't remember me from last September, but my partner and I stayed at your hotel three days while we were being outfitted with trappers' supplies. Scott Mackenzie took us beyond the railroad construction site, where we spent the fall trapping and hunting."

"By George, yes, I do, now that you mention it. We all thought you were crazy as loons to go so far beyond the construction site. But it must have turned out all right. You're back with a load of furs. Where's your partner? Went out ahead of you, did he?"

"That's part of a long story, too. Can it wait until I've washed up and had supper?"

"Goodness, yes," responded his embarrassed host. "Let's get you set up with a room. Then you'll have the best meal you've had in a long time. My Mary sure can cook."

The meal that Pat promised Barney was as good as Pat had advertised. After several helpings of mashed potatoes and roast beef, topped off with a large slice of apple pie and steaming hot coffee, Barney was ready to respond to what became an unceasing interrogation about the details surrounding Louie's disappearance. After several hours of conversation, consisting of questions from Pat and several patrons who had wandered into the barroom that also served as a dining room, the audience was ready to announce its own interpretation and verdict of what had transpired.

"What do you think happened to your partner?" asked one.

"I'll bet he's snug and warm with his Indian maiden," suggested another.

"The Indians who live in that area have never caused any problems before," offered a long-time native of Prince Rupert. "I'd be surprised if they harmed your partner."

"No, I think it was the Indians to the far north who came into the valley," protested Barney, aware that none of the occupants believed his story.

"Wait several years, and one day he'll appear as though nothing happened. Sort of Rip Van Winkle type." offered another.

"I sure wouldn't bet any money on him having been done in by the Indians," suggested yet another. "Indians north of the Hazelton area have lived peaceably with the fur traders for years."

"That may be true," responded Barney, "but I don't think the people in the wigwams were from the Hazelton area. Mackenzie told us that tribes from the far north came to the valley to hunt deer and caribou and claimed the area as their ancient hunting grounds."

Barney soon became aware that his suggestions that Louie's disappearance was due to foul play were falling on deaf ears. Satisfied that he would have to present a more convincing story to Mountie Mackenzie the next day, Barney excused himself and retired to his room for a night of badly needed rest. As he mounted the steps to his room he glanced down to the barroom where the men who had listened to his description of Louie's actions on the last days along the trapline were engaged in a dynamic discussion, speculating about his whereabouts.

Barney wondered why his account of Louie's absence made it so hard for others to accept. "They just don't know Louie the way I did," Barney reassured himself. As he pulled the down cover over his thin frame, content that from now on he would not have to stoke a campfire to keep from freezing during the night, he hoped that Louie, too, was well-fed, dry, and warm. Despite his good wishes for the welfare of his partner, he felt a twang of irritation for the behavior that had led to Louie's troubles and the difficulty that such actions now presented to Barney.

Mary's culinary skills exceeded her husband's boastful pride of her accomplishments. After a breakfast of eggs, hash browned potatoes, bacon, toast topped with homemade blackberry jam and coffee, an invigorated Barney was ready for the day's activities. His objectives were to file the report about his missing partner and then sell his furs. He realized that these two events might consume more than the few days he had allotted for their accomplishment, but as he descended the stairs leading to the front desk he was optimistic about his ability to carry out each task as he had rehearsed it prior to falling asleep the previous evening.

"Want some help with grading your furs?" called Pat as Barney was about to leave the hotel.

"What do you have in mind?" asked Barney, aware that his self-confidence often exceeded his knowledge or abilities, especially in the new venture of selling furs.

"Ole Dan Fisher has a room next to yours. He sold his furs to the Hudson Bay furrier last week. He might be able to give you some good advice so the guys that represent the fur company can't take advantage of you. Won't cost you more than a drink and maybe five bucks," suggested Pat.

"Sounds like good advice to me," replied Barney, who knew that he possessed prime furs but had no idea what prices the furs would bring.

"I'll wake him while you bring over your furs. You can spread them out right here in the lobby. Won't anybody come in here until late afternoon, if then? You can have the place all to yourselves," offered the accommodating Pat.

Barney was aware that Pat's offer was made, in part, because he was desirous of the men's company, but the overture was too good to refuse. "OK, I'll be back in ten minutes. Get Dan up, and let's see if his estimates match mine about the value of our furs."

As Barney pulled his sled of furs into the floor of the hotel lobby he was greeted by a grizzled hulk of a man, clad in woolen trousers held up by wide gray-green suspenders that stretched over a suit of long woolen underwear. He wore no shirt and his tussled hair suggested that he had been hustled downstairs without having time for his morning toilet. Barney suspected that it was the promise of early morning whiskey that had resulted in his presence on such short notice.

"Well, young feller, let's see what you got," announced the craggy old trapper as he eagerly helped Barney unload his sled.

"Mighty fine, mighty fine," he kept muttering as he ran his giant-sized hands down the length of each pelt, brushing the smooth hairs from nose to tail. "Haven't seen pelts like this in ten years. Mine were good, but these are excellent. Weather had something to do with it, but you did an excellent job of fleshing out the pelts. Bet you hung them up separately instead of piling them one on top of the other?" questioned the old veteran.

"Yep, they were all hung up to dry separately," confirmed Barney.

"Well, let's start counting," commanded Dan. "I'll tell you what I think each pelt is worth, and you can add 'em up."

With that, the two trappers worked their way through the sled full of furs. After several hours of inspection Dan announced, "Well, there you have it. Now how about my drink?"

"Coming right up. And here are ten dollars for your work. Do you have any advice about where I should sell the furs?"

"You only have two choices. Either you sell them to the Hudson Bay Company here in Rupert, or you can take them to Prince George on the train. You're in luck if you want to sell them in Rupert. The Hudson Bay Company is closing shop on December 15, so you can still catch their agent. Otherwise, you have to take them to Prince George."

"Thanks for your help. If I get the prices you quoted I'll be back, and we'll have another drink before and maybe a few more after supper," replied Barney, aware that the old trapper had done him a huge favor. Now he was equipped to appear before the fur trader as an expert instead of as the novice he had been just two hours earlier.

Barney located the office of the Hudson Fur Company several blocks from the hotel. As he entered the door he was greeted by a man dressed in a black suit, complete with a white shirt and a small black bow tie. "What can I do for you?" asked the man who Barney assumed to be the agent representing the Hudson Bay Company.

"I have some furs to sell. I thought I'd stop in here for an estimate before I head out for Prince Edward," replied Barney, now confident that he was in a position to negotiate the best possible price for his pelts.

"Well, the buying season is nearly over," countered the agent, "but I'll take a look, seeing that you have the furs right here."

"I'm only interested in cash and in U.S. dollars," demanded Barney, attempting to retain the upper hand in the negotiations. "I don't want Canadian money."

"U.S. dollars are hard to come by up here, but let's see what you have and then we can decide on the money," suggested the agent. "Place your furs up here on the table, one by one, and I'll give you my estimate."

As the work of grading the furs progressed, Barney noted that the agent kept a tally in two columns, both of which he kept hidden from Barney. However, he noted that a look of satisfaction appeared on the face of the agent as pelt after beautiful pelt was placed on the table.

"Your furs grade out well," announced the agent. "I can give you top price for most of them. My tally comes to two thousand five hundred dollars in Canadian and two thousand two hundred dollars in the United States money."

Barney was both pleased and a bit irritated at the offer. Dan had told him the furs were worth two thousand five hundred dollars in U.S. money, but Barney also realized that there was no guarantee that he could sell them for more money in Prince George. Barney had expected a lower offer, with room to negotiate from the agent's opening offer. "Do you have the money available right now?" was his query to the agent.

"Cash on the barrel head," responded the agent.

"I'll take your offer because I have some other business to take care of, but I hope you realize what a very good deal you're getting," Barney assured the agent.

"I think my offer is fair. In fact, I leave for Montreal tomorrow. My trunks, loaded with furs, are already packed and ready for the morning train. It's only because you have such fine furs that I made an exception to include them with my winter shipment. Be satisfied that we both came away with a good deal," assured the agent.

"Maybe you're right" agreed Barney as he counted the one-hundred-dollar bills that the agent placed on the counter. "Got any use for a sled? I won't be needing one until next fall."

"Just leave it near the road," suggested the agent. "One of the children will pick it up tomorrow, and by the end of the week it will be turned into the neighborhood dog sled."

Barney's next stop was at the Prince Rupert Bank, where he purchased a bank draft of one thousand dollars in his own name and another for eleven hundred dollars to be retrieved by either Louie Harris or Barney Seefeldt. In explanation to the cashier, he said, "If Louie Harris calls for the draft, you can recognize him as six feet three inches tall, with blond hair. He will have a North Dakota driver's license." The cashier assured Barney that the draft would be on file, drawing interest, until it was retrieved. The remaining one hundred dollars he converted to smaller bills, reasoning that this was sufficient cash for his fare and incidentals until he reached Grover, Wisconsin, which was his next destination.

Barney approached his next task with a heavy heart. Having delayed his upcoming mission to the very last, he now was obliged to go to the station of the Canadian Royal Mounted Police, where he hoped that Scott Mackenzie would listen to his account of Louie's disappearance and perhaps offer some encouraging advice about how to locate him. What if Scott refused to believe him, as had all the rest of the local residents? No, Scott knew Louie and would at least consider the possibility of Louie being kidnapped as a feasible explanation for his disappearance. With this assurance, Barney climbed the steps of the stately brick building and asked the man behind the desk if he could see Scott Mackenzie.

"Officer Mackenzie is not here. He's in Montreal, on furlough until next May. Can I help you?" asked the middle-aged Mountie who apparently was Mackenzie's replacement.

"I'm here to report my partner as missing," replied Barney. "Mountie Mackenzie is the one who took my partner and me to our homesteads in September. I wanted to tell him how Louie Harris disappeared, thinking that perhaps he could give me some ideas about finding him."

"I have some forms here that you'll have to complete if you want to declare your partner as missing. It's a standard form, so when you are done, hand it to me and then we can talk about when, where, how, and why you think he disappeared."

As Barney struggled with the pages of forms that the Mountie presented to him he wished that he had Louie's facility with the English language. He recalled how Louie loved to read and write, and for a moment he relived the amusement that Louie's notes had provided during the trapping season. Barney wondered if he would ever again have the chance to approach a message box somewhere in the wilderness and laugh at Louie's way of looking at life. The Mountie, peering up from his desk, sensed that Barney was having difficulty completing the forms. "Sir, can I be of help?" he offered.

"You sure can," responded Barney, who had never seen some of the words that appeared in the questions that filled the pages. "How about if I tell you what happened and you write what I tell you?"

"I think it will work better if I ask you the questions, then you answer, and I'll convert what you tell me into something that I can put on this form," suggested the Mountie.

"Sounds good to me," consented Barney, who was glad the Mountie offered to assume the responsibility of completing the forms.

After completing the papers that were designed to inform the Royal Mounted Police about the circumstances surrounding the disappearance of persons in the British Columbian wilderness, Barney could tell that he had related his story to an unsympathetic Mountie. As Barney surmised, Mountie Fitzgerald was to remain in Prince Rupert until Mackenzie returned. Being sent to Prince

Rupert, which Fitzgerald considered an outpost, after being stationed in Montreal for most of his days in uniform, was not regarded as an ideal assignment, and the Mountie was not shy about letting anyone within earshot know about it. The thought of spending the dark, cold winter months so far from civilization was especially distasteful to him because he was scheduled to retire the following summer. Mountie Fitzgerald did not appear interested or eager to help Barney solve the problem of a missing companion.

Barney now realized that any hope of obtaining assistance in his quest to locate and rescue Louie were dashed by the absence of Scott Mackenzie. "Is there anyway that you can check the other outposts to see if Louie has been seen with any of the Indian tribes that may have camped near the forts?" asked Barney.

"I'll call the stations at Kitwanga and South Hazelton to alert them about the possibility of your friend being with the Indian bands that roam the area. However, there may be a number of white men living with Indians. Once they join the tribes they blend in. It's difficult to tell a white man from an Indian when they're all dressed in furs."

"If they saw Louie Harris, they would be sure to recognize him," protested Barney. "He is six feet, three inches tall and weighs about two hundred and thirty-five pounds. He would be easy to recognize. Not many men living with Indians and not any Indians I've seen around here are that large," interjected Barney. However, he was now convinced that any effort by Mountie Fitzgerald to locate Louie would be superficial and performed only to meet the bare essentials required by Canadian law.

Frustrated and angry, Barney returned to his hotel room, where he wrote a letter to Scott Mackenzie, explaining why he believed that Louie had been the victim of foul play. He asked Scott

Mackenzie, upon his return, to read the account on the "missing persons" form that he had filed with the Mounted Police. Then he returned to the Royal Mounted Police Station and requested that Mountie Fitzgerald deliver the letter to Scott Mackenzie, or, in the event that Louie Harris passed that way prior to Mackenzie's return, to deliver the letter to Louie. Having completed his responsibilities in Prince Rupert, Barney paid his bill at the hotel, thanked his host and hostess for their accommodations and departed for the railroad depot, where he purchased a ticket that would take him to Green Bay, Wisconsin, via Prince George, Winnipeg, and Minneapolis.

As Barney waited for the afternoon train to pull into Prince Rupert he retraced his experiences, beginning with the joyful arrival of Louie and he in September. He recalled their elation at being told that their request to have homesteads far beyond the reaches of modern-day civilization had been granted. He closed his eyes and pictured the beautiful valley with the Skeena River flowing through it, a portion of which they now owned as homesteaders. The trapping experience had exceeded their wildest dreams. Both now possessed more money than either had ever thought possible. And then-the dream came to an abrupt end. Somewhere out in the vast wilderness, seemingly beyond the reach of any one inclined to rescue him, was his partner and recently his best friend. He hoped Louie was enjoying life to the fullest. Barney prayed that Louie would come to Prince Rupert and collect his check, contact him and together they could repeat this year's experiences next fall.

As Barney mounted the four steps leading to the passenger car he noted that a light snow had begun to fall, reminiscent of the snowfall that greeted him two weeks ago when he opened the cabin door to begin his quest for Louie. The engineer blew the whistle three times, indicating that the train was leaving Prince Rupert.

Barney found a seat and glanced back at the city that had been the source of such apprehension and excitement in September and now, four months later, it lay shrouded in gloom with the memory of a lost companion. A bend in the Skeena River soon hid the city from Barney's sight. The only indication that civilization existed there came from the vapor fumes that rose above the treetops, propelled there from the exhaust stacks of the lone lumber mill from which most of Prince Rupert's residents drew their livelihood. These last vestiges, too, were soon swept away by the prevailing north wind. Barney turned his gaze to the front of the train, still unaware that Prince Rupert and Louie Harris would become a memory that would haunt him the remainder of his life.

Postnote

Despite Barney's repeated attempts of locate his partner, the man known to him as Louie Harris was never seen or heard from again. After five years of calling the authorities in Prince Rupert to learn if Louie had appeared to collect his bank draft, Barney retrieved the money held jointly in their names and used it for a down payment on the farm that he purchased in Grover, Wisconsin. Barney never again visited his homestead in British Columbia, which after a period of three years without improvements, reverted to Crown land, under the auspices of the Land Management Office in British Columbia.

Barney Seefeldt died in Grover, Wisconsin, on December 14, 1973, on the farm where he resided for the remainder of his life. Aside from building submarines in Manitowoc, Wisconsin, during World War II, he never again traveled far from his farm. However, his adventures in British Columbia remained vividly in his memory, brought to the forefront during hunting and fishing trips with family and friends in Marinette and Vilas Counties, in northeastern Wisconsin.

Edwards Brothers, Inc.
Thorofare, NJ USA
July 5, 2011